T0196687

BOOK LIST OF MARY GOLOVERSIC

<u>Books for adults and teens:</u>
Three novels (published prior to 2019): Iron Heart, Living
    on the Edge, Raging Fire
True stories: I Married a Troll, Joys of Raising Boys,
    Woman in the Well, Death of a Mother
Self-help with God books: Diary of a Drunk, Games of a
    Gambler, Changing, God's Team, Scents for
    Women (Minutes for Men and Tips for Teens)
Success System books (godly success)—Successful Starts,
    Successful Love, Successful Forgiveness,
    Successful Communication, Successful Help,
    Success Club Manual, Success Memo, Travel to
    Success

<u>Books for children:</u>
Stubby the Stubborn Kitten (part of the Success System)
Stubby el Gatito Obstinato (condensed English/Spanish)
12 Critter books—Water Gang, Capture Camera, Scamper
    the Shy Cat, Mischievous Mopsy, Candy the One-
    eared Cat, Bully Chase, Adventures of Boo Boy,
    Crandon the Curious Cat, Whiskers Watches,
    Walking the Dogs, Little Pets, Pet Parade

GAMES OF A GAMBLER

Mary Goloversic

authorHOUSE®

AuthorHouse™
1663 Liberty Drive
Bloomington, IN 47403
www.authorhouse.com
Phone: 1 (800) 839-8640

© 2020 Mary Goloversic. All rights reserved.

No part of this book may be reproduced, stored in a retrieval system, or
transmitted by any means without the written permission of the author.

Note: The author grants permission to copy the pages marked for copying for use at
        Stub Club meetings and for other noncommercial Christian purposes.
        If you copy these pages, be sure to include the copyright information.

Published by AuthorHouse 04/13/2020

ISBN: 978-1-4685-3642-3 (sc)

Print information available on the last page.

Any people depicted in stock imagery provided by Getty Images are models,
and such images are being used for illustrative purposes only.
Certain stock imagery © Getty Images.

Bible quotations from the King James Version of the Bible by the National Bible Press in 1957.

This book is printed on acid-free paper.

Because of the dynamic nature of the Internet, any web addresses or links contained in
this book may have changed since publication and may no longer be valid. The views
expressed in this work are solely those of the author and do not necessarily reflect the
views of the publisher, and the publisher hereby disclaims any responsibility for them.

HOW TO BUY MORE BOOKS BY THE AUTHOR
<u>Buy the books at bookstores or other stores that sell books in USA and UK</u> (if
they are not in stock, they can be ordered at most bookstores through Ingram—
Day Spring division; might have to use the back order procedure)
<u>Order the books direct from Author House</u>
        By phone hotline, 1-888-290-7715
        By computer, www.authorhouse.com
        By mail, Author House, 1663 Liberty Drive, Suite 200, Bloomington, IN 47403

TABLE OF CONTENTS

The parole board had just met and Bob had been interviewed. Now he sat in his prison cell with hope in his heart, yet despair too. He was bent over with his head down.

He'd had his hopes raised before. Then an incident out in the exercise yard had set him back. He'd accidentally grabbed a hat owned by a member of one of the prison gang members, thinking it was his own hat. One of the gang members saw him take it. It was a hot day and tempers had risen with the mercury in the thermometer. A small fight had erupted. He hadn't fought back, but just being in an altercation was enough for a bad report for the parole board. His request for parole had been rejected.

This time his record was clean. It was time for freedom—he hoped.

No longer would he be confined to the small cell, the hard cot, the open toilet. No longer would he have to fear hot tempers and sharp objects. No longer would he have to listen to curses and threats or the snoring of dozens of men. No longer would he hear the steps and shouts of the guards. No more would his personal letters be read or would he speak through mesh dividers when he had an occasional visitor. He wouldn't have the institutional food, the monotonous repetitive schedule, or the same style clothing every day.

Yet what would his future be like? He'd lost his home, his business, his savings, his family—all went with his trips to the casino.

He was part-owner of a prosperous used car lot, and

then the recession had come. Sales dropped, but the business survived, because some people could still afford the lower-priced used cars. His business partner went to auto auctions to procure the cars. He, himself, took car of the books. He wasn't satisfied with the slow, but steady, low income.

The casino offered him so much hope. At first he just used part of the household money. Then he dug into his children's college funds. Then he used up the savings account and mortgaged the house. Then the house went and he had to rent. The two good cars went, and he had to lease a car. He covered the real reason for his losses by saying he preferred to rent a home and lease a car as there was no upkeep on them.

He fooled his family and business partner, but he couldn't fool himself. He became desperate. Little by little, he fixed the business books. He embezzled, bit by bit, then more and more until the business faced bankruptcy.

Then came the audit of the business books, and the truth came out.

He had lost everything by gambling, but he wasn't the only one to suffer. His gambling hurt his family and his business partner and his family.

Now, as he sat in his prison cell waiting for his freedom, he wondered, *What will freedom bring?*

Chapter 2

Bob heard the many-barred door click into lock behind him as a guard escorted him out of the prison and the door to freedom. His parole had been approved. A friend had arrived to pick him up.

It was wonderful to see the sky, feel the warmth of the sun on his face, and inhale the fresh air.

"It's so great to be outside. Three years behind bars! What a waste."

"I'm glad to be with you on this happy day," said Tom. "It's too bad you have to stay at the halfway house, though."

"It'll be better than being behind bars. It seems so strange to be out, though."

"I want to take you out to lunch before I drop you off, Bob. What would you like—fast food or a buffet?"

"Maybe a little restaurant. I'm not sure I want to be around a lot of people yet."

"I passed a diner on the way in. We'll go there."

*   *   *

Sitting in a booth in the back of the diner, Bob scanned the menu. He hadn't seen a menu in three years. The prices had increased, but the foods were the same. A hot beef sandwich and a piece of apple pie sounded like a feast to Bob.

Yet he wondered if the waitress realized he was an ex-convict. Tom had brought him a pair of casual slack and a knit shirt, but he knew his skin was pale from being inside so much. He felt awkward speaking—even to give his order to the waitress. Tom didn't seem to notice.

"How does it feel to be in a restaurant, Bob? Guess you won't miss prison food."

"No," replied Bob, hoping nobody heard the word, "prison." Bob didn't answer the question about is feelings about being in a restaurant. All of a sudden, he turned inward. He wasn't ready to face the outside world. At least he wouldn't know anybody in this city. It was hundreds of miles from his home town.

* * *

Lunch seemed to last forever, but finally they finished their food. Tom put a top on the table, paid the bill, and they left to go to the halfway house.

Bob looked around as they drove across town. He'd live here for three years, but hadn't seen the city. It was dark when he was brought to the prison, and he hadn't left the prison compound since then.

The halfway house was a rambling one-story brick building surrounded by grass and sidewalks. There were a few commercial buildings nearby, but the halfway house was set apart. A few men were walking along the sidewalks.

Tom rang the doorbell.

A man let them in and said he'd take Bob to the office.

"I guess we part company here, Bob," said Tom. He reached and shook Bob's hand. "I won't get back here to see you much—it's too far to drive often, but I'll write and phone."

"Thanks for everything, Tom. Your kindness means a lot to me, especially today."

Tom turned and walked out the door. Bob knew Tom had to return home to his family and job, yet he felt deserted.

Tom turned and walked out the door. Bob knew Tom had to return home to his family and job, yet he felt deserted.

Chapter 3

Bob entered the office cautiously. This person wouldn't be a prison warden, but he was in charge of Bob's life, and Bob knew little about life in a halfway house.

A tall strong-looking man rose from his desk chair and extended his hand to Bob. For a moment, Bob hesitated and then shook hands.

"Welcome. You must be Bob. We've been expecting you. I'm Joe."

"Glad to meet you, sir," replied Bob, still aware of prison protocol.

"Have a seat," said Joe, returning to his chair. "Would you like a cup of coffee?"

"No, thanks," said Bob. He knew his nerves were already on edge without caffeine.

"We're glad you chose Success House as your halfway house. As you already know, we have a Bible-based program here. You will be expected to participate in the activities whether or not you are a Christian. Are you comfortable committing to this type of program?"

"Yes. I'm willing to go along with your ways."

"I'm glad to hear that. Willingness is a crucial aspect of using the Success House program. There are some forms for you to fill out. You can fill out these papers at the table in the lobby," said Joe, handing Bob a clipboard with the forms and a pen.

*   *   *

As Bob sat at the table filling out the forms, he took a few moments to look around. There were a few men in the lobby—some chatting, some reading the bulletin board announcements.

He saw a list of rules on the wall near him. At the top, there was "No smoking" and "No alcohol." He'd have to read the rules carefully. He didn't want to do anything that would get him booted out of the halfway house or ruin his parole.

There were forms for health history, previous jobs, and much more. Bob knew the prison information had been sent on ahead. Supposedly no dangerous people were allowed here.

Bob thought to himself, *At least I'm not a murderer.*

Then he paused in his thoughts. *I'm not a murderer, but I destroyed my marriage and my chance to be a father. I am a thief—"embezzler" is just a fancy word for "thief." I'm a failure.*

Then Bob jolted himself out of his discouraging thoughts. There were forms to be filled out, and he didn't want to start out his stay here at the halfway house in trouble for not following directions. There weren't prison cells here, but Bob knew there would be strict discipline.

*   *   *

Half an hour later, Bob turned in his completed forms to Joe who looked them over and nodded his head in approval. Joe had Bob sign two copies of the rules, agreeing to obey them—a copy for the office file and a copy for Bob.

"I have someone to show you to your room and then give

you a tour of the building. Supper is at five and then you'll get on schedule with the rest of the men.

"Thank you, sir." Bob backed out of the room and bumped into the man entering the doorway. Bob jumped aside with a look of fear. He remembered what had happened when he bumped someone at prison—he'd gotten a black eye. Then he remembered he wasn't in prison. Quickly he muttered, "I'm sorry," and hung his head.

The other man just chuckled. "Bumping into me is like bumping into a sack of potatoes." The tall man had a big belly and a big smile. "I'm Herbert, but just call me 'Herb.' I'm your roommate. Follow me."

After going down several hallways, they entered a bright room. On each side of the room, there was a chest of drawers, a closet, and a twin bed with real mattress! Below the double window were two desks with lamps and chairs. The floor was carpeted, there was a clock on the wall, and the window had colorful plaid curtains that matched the bedspreads. An extra blanket was folded neatly at the foot of each bed. *Luxury!* thought Bob.

Herb could understand Bob's joy at having a bedroom instead of a prison cell, but he didn't make any comment on it. Instead he said, "We'll go down to the clothes room where you can pick out your clothing. After you do that and put the clothes away, I'll give you a tour of the building before supper."

*　　　*　　　*

Bob was amazed at the array of clothes—no blue prison outfits!

The clothes were sorted according to type and size, but there was a variety of colors and styles from which to choose. Bob felt overwhelmed. He hadn't chosen clothing for three years. Herb steered Bob to the proper sizes of underwear, socks, jeans, slacks, shirts, sweaters, sweatshirts, and jackets. Then he opened a closet and told Bob to choose a suit in his size.

"A suit? Whatever do I need a suit for?"

"We're required to dress up and attend church on Sundays. You'll go to church with the entire group of men on Sunday."

Bob looked at the row of suits. He thought to himself, *I haven't worn a suit since the terrible day of my trial.*

He chose a suit. Herb took the stack of clothes, Bob carried the suit, and they headed back to their room.

Herb turned to Bob and said, "I'll pick up a toothbrush, comb, and razor for you. The bathroom for our unit is at the end of the hall. You'll find toothpaste and soap at the sink and bath towels, soap, and shampoo near the showers. Showers are required every day. No head lice here!"

Chapter 4

Bob woke up early. His first thought was, *Where am I?* The sounds weren't the sounds of his prison cell.

Then he realized he was in the halfway house. He relaxed and enjoyed the comfort of a real mattress.

The doorknob turned, and Bob sat up with a start. It was just Herb returning from the shower.

With a grin, Herb said, "Rise and shine. It's Saturday and time to change the sheets before breakfast. Clean sheets are on a cart in the hall and there's a laundry cart for dirty sheets. You'll have time for your shower, too."

*   *   *

Breakfast was just a bowl of cold cereal. With a fast breakfast, the men had time to clean their rooms before going their assorted ways.

Brooms, dustpans, mop buckets, mops, vacuums, window cleaner, and cleaning rags were brought out. Everyone pitched in. Within a few hours, bedrooms, halls, and bathrooms had a clean smell. The foyer, library, kitchen, dining room, and recreation room were all shiny clean.

The men had a quick lunch of sandwiches and fruit.

The men who had lived in the halfway house for many weeks and had proved themselves responsible were free to leave the house. Some of the more recent residents were limited to the ends of the house's sidewalks. Bob knew he was restricted to the house for a few weeks, unless accompanied by one of the house workers. This restriction disappointed Bob a little, but not near as much as the bars of his prison cell.

Herb said some of the guys were going to a local baseball game, accompanied by several house workers. "Want to come with us?" he invited,

Bob looked amazed. "Am I allowed?"

"Yes," replied Herb. I checked at the office before I asked you."

"Great. I'll be glad to go—just to be outside!"

*   *   *

However, Bob's euphoria was short-lived. When he got to the ball field and saw the crowd in the bleachers, he wished he was back in the confines of the house, safe from the stares of a crowd. He felt like everyone was staring at him and labeling him an ex-con. His heard beat faster.

As a group of men settled themselves high in the last row of bleachers, Bob felt better—surrounded by his housemates and with no people behind him to stare at him. Instead he could stare at the people below him on the bleachers and out on the field.

He saw the men in baseball uniforms warming up by throwing balls to each other. He saw children moving around below; he guessed the parents hoped their children would run off some energy before sitting down to watch the game. He heard the voices of the crowd, but clearly heard only a few words.

Bob began to relax. He was outside in the sunshine with

only the ball field fence around the area, and it had open gates and no barbed wire. Bob breathed in the fresh air and watched the white clouds in the blue sky. His heartbeat slowed down to normal.

The game began. The encouraging shouts and cheers rose from the lively fans—voices so different from the critical and sometimes angry shouts of prisoners. Bob settle in to enjoy his first full day of freedom.

Chapter 5

It was Friday night—game night at Success House.

After everyone scraped their dishes and set them on the counter, some men ran the dishwasher, some put away the clean dishes, some put out the trash, some returned to the tables to put away the salt, pepper, catsup, sugar, cream, milk, and coffee. Then one person at each table washed the table and someone else dried it. Several men cleaned the floors. Soon the kitchen and dining room were clean.

Games were taken out of a storage cupboard and placed on the tables. The men wandered around the dining room until they found a game that caught their interest and then sat at that table, waiting for others to join them.

Bob was hesitant. These games definitely weren't like the games as the casino. Then Herb asked him if he liked to do crossword puzzles. Bob did. Then Herb steered him to a table with a "Scrabble" game and left Bob there. Herb then wandered around to choose a game for himself.

Bob felt anxious. Years ago, before he let gambling take over his life, he'd played "Scrabble" with his wife and, seeing the game, brought back happy memories, but then came the sense of loss, knowing they had a legal separation.

Soon three other men joined him and he had no more time to dwell on sad thoughts. The game began, along with the challenges to look up questionable words in the dictionary.

The next few hours passed quickly, and Bob enjoyed the diversion of the fun game.

*   *   *

At nine o'clock, someone announced the game time was over and quiet time began. Some men headed to the small library to choose a book, some read newspapers in the lounge, some returned to their rooms to write letters, read, or do some quiet task.

Bob headed to the library and chose a novel. When he got back to his room, he saw Herb at his desk reading his Bible and taking notes.

Herb looked up and saw the perplexed look on Bob's face. "I'm doing homework for a Bible study offered at one of the churches."

"I thought only priests and preachers studied the Bible," said Bob.

"God gave us the Bible so everyone could get to know Him and learn how to obey Him and please Him. Studying the Bible helps me understand it better," answered Herb. "It brings me closer to God—helps me to know Him better."

Bob looked doubtful, but Herb encouraged him. "I'm learning a little more every week. God doesn't expect us to know everything in the Bible. He just wants us to be willing to listen to Him as He talks to us through His words in the Bible. There is a Bible in your desk."

Bob glanced at his desk. "There are pens and paper in the

drawer," said Herb. "Tape, staplers, scissors, and other office supplies are in a cabinet in the library."

"I guess I'll just read this novel for now, but thanks for all the information."

"If you like to read in bed, you can turn in any time. There's nothing else on the schedule until tomorrow. You might want to read the information on the bulletin board sometime. We have a regular schedule Monday through Friday, but Saturday and Sunday are more flexible, except for Sunday church an attendance and lunch there. If a church has a fellowship luncheon, we can stay for it."

"I guess I'll check out the bulletin board and then read."

*　　　*　　　*

The bulletin board information answered a lot of Bob's unspoken questions.

The schedule included group sessions, chores, outings, sports. There were also special speakers on employment, budgeting, and all sorts of subjects. A Success Club was listed, too. Bob thought to himself, *A Success Club is not for me. I'm a failure.*

Bob saw a few posters of music groups coming to entertain and worship. The thought of hearing uplifted him.

On that thought, he slowly walked back to the bathroom to shower. He enjoyed every step of the way, feeling so free, even within the walls of the halfway house.

Chapter 6

Bob woke up early. His first thought was, *Where am I?* The sounds weren't the sounds of his prison cell.

Then he realized he was in the halfway house. He relaxed and enjoyed the comfort of a real mattress.

The doorknob turned, and Bib sat up with a start. It was just Herb returning from the shower.

With a grin, Herb said, "Rise and shine. It's Saturday and time to change the sheets before breakfast. Clean sheets are on a cart in the hall and there's a laundry cart for dirty sheets. You'll have time for your shower, too."

*　　　　*　　　　*

Breakfast was just a bowl of cold cereal. With a fast breakfast, the men had time to clean their rooms before going their assorted ways.

Brooms, dustpans, mop buckets, mops, vacuums, window cleaner, and cleaning rags were brought out. Everyone pitched in. Within a few hours, bedrooms, halls, and bathrooms had a fresh clean smell. The foyer, library, kitchen, dining room, and recreation room were all shiny clean.

The men had a quick lunch of sandwiches and fruit.

The men who had lived in the halfway house for many weeks and had proved themselves responsible were free to leave the house. Some of the more recent residents were limited to the ends of the house's sidewalks. Bob knew he was restricted to the house for a few weeks, unless accompanied by one of the house workers. This restriction disappointed Bob a little, but not near as much as the bars on his prison cell.

Herb said some of the boys were going to a local baseball game, accompanied by several house workers. "Want to come with us?" he invited.

Bob looked amazed. "Am I allowed?"

"Yes," replied Herb. I checked at the office before I asked you."

"Great. I'll be glad to go—just to be outside!"

*   *   *

However, Bob's euphoria was short-lived. When he got to the ball field and saw the crowd in the bleachers, he wished he was back in the confines of the house, safe from the stares of a crowd. He felt like everyone was staring at him and labeling him an ex-con. His heart beat faster.

As the group of men settled themselves high up in the last row of bleachers, Bob felt better—surrounded by his housemates and with no people behind him to stare at him. Instead he could stare at the people below him on the bleachers and out on the field.

He was the men in baseball uniforms warming up by throwing balls to each other. He saw children moving around below; he guessed the parents hoped their children would run off some energy before sitting down to watch the game. He heard the voices of the crowd, but clearly heard only a few words.

Bob began to relax. He was outside in the sunshine with

only the ball field fence around the area, and it had open gates and no barbed wire. Bob breathed in the fresh air and watched the white clouds in the blue sky. His heartbeat slowed down to normal.

The game began. The encouraging shouts and cheers rose from the lively fans—voices so different from the critical and sometimes angry shouts of prisoners. Bob settled in to enjoy his first full-day of freedom.

Chapter 7

As Herb had told Bob, Sunday mornings meant going to church. Getting into several vans, the men went to a Bible church located on the edge of the city. It wasn't a huge mega-church, but it was large enough to include seating for the men from Success House. Bob noticed that the pew racks held Bibles as well as hymnals, and the bulletin handed to him included a study note page for the message.

Bob had gone to church on Christmas and Easter, but seldom the rest of the year. The churches he had attended had no Bibles in the pews.

He had been warmly welcomed at the door by greeters and also by some of the other people. A lot of talking had gone on before the service, but, at the sound of the piano prelude, the voices gradually hushed.

Like other churches he'd attended, the service started with hymns and prayers. Then there was group reading from the Bible. Herb had brought his own Bible and shared it with Bob. This was new to Bob—he'd never read a Bible before.

The message was about giving forgiveness to people. The pastor asked the people to look up Ephesians 4:32. "And be ye kind one to another, tenderhearted, forgiving one another, even as God for Christ's sake hath forgiven you."

Herb again shared his Bible with Bob. Herb also pointed out that the verse was quoted on the study note page in the bulletin. The pastor stressed that the word "give" is in forgiveness, that forgiveness is a gift you give with no strings attached—no "ifs" or "buts." For example, he said, "Don't say, 'I'll forgive you, <u>if</u> you forgive me.'

"Don't say, 'I'll forgive you, <u>but</u> you have to promise never to do that again.' You simply say, 'I forgive you.' There should be no words of criticism, no words of condemnation."

The pastor included many quotations, and Herb looked them up when the references were given; Herb also took notes. Bob continued to listen intently. This sort of forgiveness was new to him. Hearing the Scriptures quoted and comments by the pastor, Bob thought, *This gives me a lot to absorb and think about.*

The congregation had planned what they called a "fellowship lunch," so everyone was invited to attend. It was "potluck," so there was quite an array of salads, casseroles, and desserts on the two long serving tables. Bob hadn't seen that much of a variety of food since he had entered prison. It was like a holiday banquet to him. The people were talking and joking and laughing.

The pastor gave a shrill whistle, and everyone went silent while he gave the blessing for the food. Then lines formed on each side of the serving tables. As the plates were filled, people moved on to the round tables to sit down and eat. The residents of the halfway house mingled with the members of the congregation at the various tables.

Herb and Bob chose a table with two couples at it.

Conversation went well, helped along by Herb's outgoing personality. There was talk about the weather, ballgame, and morning message. Bob was afraid he wouldn't fit in with the church-going people, but, with the easy conversation, he was even able to add a few of his opinions.

All too soon, it seemed to Bob, it was time to "return home" to the halfway house. He was surprised that he was already calling it his home. Prison had never seemed like home, though it had housed him for three years.

Chapter 8

"Welcome to Success Club, Bob," said the house worker.

We meet every morning from nine until eleven, Monday through Friday. We don't go through an entire Success Club meeting, but we do cover a topic a day. Everyone is required to attend these morning meetings to learn to be a success in daily living, both in and out of the Success House. Success, as we use the word here, is being the person God wants you to be.

Success House is a halfway house for men coming out of prison, coming off of alcohol and drugs, coming out of hospital psych units, and all sorts of situations, such as being out-of-work due to a broken leg or being homeless.

There is a women's and children's division of Success House across town. That includes women with all sorts of troubles—women with the same problems that face men here and women with unplanned pregnancies and injuries from abuse. There is also a teen division there. There are Success Clubs there for women and teens and Stub Clubs for children.

These halfway houses are called Success Houses, because they stress using the eight steps to success both at Success Houses and beyond. Success Club is the core of learning how to become a success here. You'll be using the Bible and the five main success books.

In Success Club, we cover a topic at every meeting. There are 182 topics in the five main success books, so they cover about nine months, if you stay here that long. Everyone progresses at different rates, so dome leave before the nine months are up and some stay longer—up to a year.

A year is the longest time you can stay here, because many other men are waiting to live here.

The information used at this meeting will probably all be new to you, Bob, but it will soon be easy for you to participate. Once a month, we have a Success Workshop for newcomers. There's one coming up next week. That will provide you with a good introduction to the *Success System*. Also, here is an "8-Steps to Success" pamphlet for you; it has all the basics in it.

Now we'll begin the meeting.

*　　　　*　　　　*

Bob felt a bit confused over the next two hours, but he didn't feel uncomfortable. Everything was in the Success book and the club handbook, and Herb helped him look up that day's Bible quote. As Bob wrote down that day's information on a note card, it started to make sense to him. When he finished writing, he again looked at the cover of the success pamphlet. It said, "Want to be successful? You can. Today!" *Today?* Bob questioned himself. *Was it possible?* The group had worked on a success topic today. Was that HIS start? Didn't he already have success in his business before the economy got bad and he began to gamble?

*　　　　*　　　　*

The day passed quickly. Before dinner Bob had time to look over the eight-steps pamphlet. He read that success is being God's king of person. That was something to consider. He had always felt that success was having money, a good job or business, a big home and luxury car, prestige power, a winning personality. Bob thought, *Have I been wrong in my thinking?* It was something to consider.

Chapter 9

A week passed quickly passed—seeming to pass so much faster than a week in prison with its rigid routine and the boredom and loneliness, even in the midst of the prison population.

It was the day of the Success Workshop, held on a Saturday. It would take all day. Bob yearned to be outside, as he had been at the ball game, but he knew he was in the Success House to recover, not to have fun.

There were only two other people at the workshop—all newcomers to the Success House.

Reading the success pamphlet had helped Bob prepare for the workshop, but the in-depth coverage of the eight steps to success gave fuller insights into the eight-step plan.

Bob had heard of Success Club meetings before living at the Success House, but he knew little about them. He had been a successful businessman and thought he didn't need to go to a Success Club. Now he knew there was much more to learn. The club meetings not only included Scriptures, but also stressed the applications of the Scriptures to daily living.

During the five Success Club meetings the week before, Bob had begun to learn and apply the eight steps to success. He could repeat the steps from memory at the meetings.

1. Read Bible truths
2. Recognize lies
3. Repent
4. Replace

5. Love
6. Forgive
7. Communicate
8. Help

As Bob tuned into the words of the workshop 1 and absorbed the information in the workshop booklet, he realized how much there was to learn about becoming a success.

Just reading the list of 182 success topics provided challenges for him. *How will I ever learn it all?* he asked himself.

Then Bob remembered how the club leader had said it took months to learn how to be a success. He could learn gradually, at his own rate of progress. He already had learned a lot. He realized nobody was perfect; everyone could become better and better for God.

He read and reread the success pamphlet. It gave him an overall look at how to be a success.

Chapter 10

Two weeks had already passed. Bob had learned the details of the eight steps to success. Ten topics had been covered at the Success Club meetings. Now he was scheduled to start going to a Success House counselor for individual counseling, a half-hour twice a week—Tuesdays and Thursdays. Bob entered the counselor's office cautiously, not knowing what to expect.

The man stood up from his desk as Bob entered. "Glad to see you, Bob. I'm Jim Jackson. Just call me "Jim."" He extended his hand and clasped Bob's for a warm strong shake.

Bob was surprised at the strength of the tall slim man.

"Have a seat," said Jim, motioning to a chair across from the desk. "I've already looked over you intake form, but I'd rather hear you tell me about yourself and how you got to this point in your life."

"As you know, the economy got bad. I own a used-car lot jointly with my cousin. Sales dropped, and I started to supplement my income with casino winnings. Then I got on a losing streak and took money from the business to cover my losses and keep gambling. I continued to lose and an auditor caught my personal withdrawals. I spent three years in prison. The bad economy sure hurt me. Those crooked politicians sure ruined my life."

"Why did you choose this halfway house instead of returning to your own city?"

"I couldn't face my family yet—my wife, my kids, and my cousin—my business partner."

"What do you expect from this Success House instead of a halfway house near your home?"

"Time to adjust."

"You just consider this a stopover to pass time."

"I don't mean to offend you, but I don't think I need counseling. I know what to do—stop gambling and concentrate on rebuilding the business."

"As you know, counseling is required here. You have the knowledge to rebuild the business. We hope to provide you with wisdom to rebuild your life. Nobody is perfect, but we all can improve, including me."

Bob was surprised at the counselor's humility. He expected someone who would claim to know all the answers. Jim further demonstrated his modesty with his next words.

"I have had years of training to counsel and years of counseling experience, but it is God's wisdom that will direct you to success."

"I know I can successfully rebuild the business."

"Yes, Bob, with your business experience you probably can. I'm talking about a different kind of success—being God's kind of person."

"I went to services at the prison some Sundays. I went to church occasionally before prison, too. I don't think I need to learn more about religion."

"Have you ever read the Bible?"

"I didn't have to. The ministers did that. They read from the Bible on Sundays."

"Here at Success House, we base the counseling on the Bible. We don't teach you more about 'religion," but we do help you learn more about God. We want you to understand God's wisdom, because God's words in the Bible lead to success."

Jim took time to read two Scriptures.

"This book of the law shall not depart out of thy mouth; but thou shalt meditate therein day and night, that thou mayest observe to do according to all that is written therein: for then thou shalt make thy way prosperous, and then thou shalt have good success." (Joshua 1:8)

"So shall my word be that goeth forth out of my mouth: it shall not return unto me void, but it shall accomplish that which I please, and it shall prosper in the thing whereto I sent it." (Isaiah 55:11)

"Bob, do you believe those words?"

"I don't know. I never thought about that. The Bible is a good book. I don't know if all the stories are factual."

"I appreciate your honesty, Bob." Jim handed Bob a long narrow paper with Psalm 119:60 written on it. "I want you to look up just that one verse. I see you brought the pen and Bible from your desk as requested. That Bible is yours to keep. It's a gift from Success House."

"Thank you," said Bob.

"I'll help you find that verse, and you can mark it— underline it—in ink and put the paper with the Scripture on it in your Bible as a bookmark."

"You want me to underline in the Bible?" asked Bob in surprise.

"Yes. Underlining will help you remember it and find it again."

The two men looked up the verse, and Bob underlined the quotation.

"Thy word is true from the beginning: and every one of thy righteous judgments endureth for ever." (Psalm 119:60)

Then Jim said, "We'll pray for a moment. 'Dear God, thank you for bringing Bob here to Success House. Please help him as he lives here and guide Him as He reads Your words in the Bible. I pray in Jesus' Name, amen.'"

Standing up, Jim ended the session with a smile and another handshake, saying, "Over the next two days, read beyond verse 160 to the end of the chapter and all of the next two chapters. Read them at least once a day—today, Wednesday, and Thursday. Then I'll see you on Thursday."

*　　　　*　　　　*

When Bob returned to his room, it was empty. He sat at his desk and read the assigned verses. One verse really hit home for him.

"In my distress I cried unto the Lord, and he heard me." (Psalm 120:1)

Bob thought, *Would God hear ME, an ex-con?* The thought troubled him.

Chapter 11

Counseling sessions seemed to come quickly. Time seemed to pass so much faster here as Success House than the slow moving days of monotonous prison life

"Welcome back, Bob," greeted Jim while remaining seated.

"Hello, Jim," replied Bob as he sat down.

"Today I'd like to begin with prayer." Jim bowed his head and closed his eyes and Bob followed suit.

"Dear God, Thank You for bringing Jim and me together. Please help us today as we study your word together. In Jesus' Name, amen."

Looking up, Jim said, "Let's look at that verse from last week." Jim flicked through the pages of his Bible looking for Psalm 119:160.

Bob opened his Bible to the page with the bookmark and the underlined verse.

"Let's read the verse together again, Bob."

They read in unison.

"Thy word is true from the beginning: and every one of thy righteous judgments endureth for ever."

"Bob, I want you to look at the first words of the verse, 'Thy word is true.' Last week you said that you weren't sure if all of the Bible is true. Do you still think that?"

"Well, the verse says God's words are true, and I shouldn't argue with God."

"You still don't sound sure," commented Jim.

"If that's so, then how would you pick and choose what is true and what is not?" asked Jim.

"I don't know."

"Let me read you a few other verses. Jim read Hebrews 6:18 and then asked, "Did you notice the words, '…it was impossible for God to lie….'?"

"But the Bible was written by men. Maybe the men just made up some of the Bible," responded Bob.

"Let me read to you from II Timothy 3:16-17. Jim paused and looked up the verse.

"'All scripture is given by inspiration of God, and is profitable for doctrine, for reproof, for correction, for instruction in righteousness: That the man of God may be perfect, throughly furnished unto all good works.' Note that the quotation says "all scripture," not just part of the Scriptures. God inspired the writers of the Bible, guided the authors as they wrote all the books of the Bible.

I know some of this information is new to you, but, as you continue reading the Bible, you will understand more and more. Bible by bit, God's truths will begin to blend together, showing you that it is all true. None of it is false; none of it is contradictory."

Jim paused to let the words sink into Bob's mind. Then he asked, "What did you think about what you read in the Bible over the last few days?"

"One of the verses said that the person cried to God and God heard him. Will God listen to me, an ex-con?" asked Jim.

"God is everywhere, and He is a good listener. He does

want us to confess our sins as we talk to Him. John 9:31 tells us, "'Now we know that God heareth not sinners: but if any man be a worshipper of God, and doeth his will, him he heareth.' If you confess your past sins to God, He will listen to you. God also wants us—you and me   to accept Jesus to pay for our sins. I know you have read the success pamphlet given to you at the Success Club meetings. Look it up this week and read the back page. We'll talk about that next week. This week I want you to learn how much God loves you."

"Can God love ex-cons?"

"Yes. John 3:16 tells us that God loves everyone. Today we'll read I John, chapter 4, that tells about how much God loves us."

The rest of the half-hour passed quickly. Jim closed the session with prayer. "Dear God, thank You for loving us, even before we loved You. Help Bob to know how much You love him. I pray in Jesus' Name, amen."

Bob stood up to leave and Jim reminded him, "Look up your success pamphlet and read the back of it every day until your next session on Tuesday. Also, ask your roommate to look up the verses on the back of the pamphlet with you. Herb has been here for many months, so he's prepared to help you."

<u>Chapter 12</u>

It was quiet time, almost bed time, and Bob and Herb were in their room, each sitting at his own desk.

"My counselor told me to ask you to help me look up the verses on the back of the success pamphlet."

"Sure," said Herb with a big smile. "Have you read the Bible before?"

"Not until I came to Success House. I had heard the Scriptures read at church, but had never read a Bible."

Herb dropped his head in sad thoughts and than looked up as Bob with a serious look on his face. "I've read the Bible since I was a child. My parents took me to church every Sunday. I became a Christian when I was twelve. After I graduated and went off to college, I stopped going to church and started to go to parties—wild parties with lots of beer. One night I was driving back to college with some friends in my car. I was drunk and speeding and cause a car accident that killed the other driver. That's how I ended up in prison and then here at Success House. It was a real wake-up call for me—at the expense of another person's life. I'll never forget that night, but since I came here, I got a new start, and that bad memory is receding some. My counselor told me that, in time, the nightmares and flashbacks will lessen. I'll never forget that night, but life is becoming better every day."

Bob was shocked. "You seem such a happy good person, Herb. I'd never have guessed he troubles you've had."

"I caused my own troubles, Bob, but I've returned to God, and I have the joy of Jesus in my heart. That's what you see in my smile." Herb gave Bob a big smile. "Now let's look at that success pamphlet."

Together the two men started to look up the verses on the back of the success pamphlet in both of their Bibles.

Herb noticed that Bob kept searching in his Bible. "Bob, if all this is new to you, look in the front of the Bible. There's a list of the books of the Bible there with the page numbers to find them. All of these are separate books. When they are all put together, they form the Bible."

Bob turned to the list. "That's great, Herb. Now I don't feel so lost trying to find verses."

Herb added, "If you look at the list, you'll se that the Bible is divided into two parts, the Old Testament covers the times before Christ was Born and the New Testament starts with the birth of Christ."

"That sure simplifies things for me. Thanks, Herb."

The two men together read aloud the verses.

"...the gospel...how Christ died for our sins according to the scriptures: And that he was buried, and that he rose again on the third day according to the scriptures: And that he was seen...of above five hundred brethren at once..." (I Corinthians 15:1,3-6)

"For God so loved the world, that he gave his only begotten Son, that whosoever believeth in him should not perish, but have everlasting life." (John 3:16)

Then Herb read the question near the top of the pamphlet. "'Have you accepted Jesus as YOUR Savior in payment for YOUR sins?'"

Herb asked Bob, "Is your answer 'yes' or 'no'?"

Bob replied, "I've never had anyone ask me that question before."

"Then let's read the prayer on this page silently."

"Have you ever heard a prayer like that?" questioned Herb.

"I've never heard or read a prayer like that," answered Bob.

"Would you like to me to tell you how I gave a prayer like that?" asked Herb.

"Sure," said Bob.

"When I was a boy, I often heard prayers like that at church, usually at the end of a service. When I was twelve, I finally realized that going to church wouldn't get me to heaven. I said and did hurtful things. I was a sinner. Romans 3:23 says, 'For all have sinned, and come short of the glory of God…'

"I could never be good enough to get into heaven. I couldn't make myself perfect to live with God. It was then that I realized Jesus had died on the cross to pay for MY sins, not only for the sins of others.

"The next Sunday when I went to church and the pastor invited anyone to go to his office after church to pray for salvation, I went forward. He talked to me in his office, and I prayed a prayer like the one on the back of the pamphlet that you and I just read. I used my own words and the pastor prayed with me.

"A feeling of real peace came over me.

"The pastor read me some Bible verses that told me I was a child of God and that the Holy Spirit lived in me.

"Would you like to pray that prayer now?"

"No. It's all too new to me. My mind can't seem to absorb it all. I need to understand more of what this is all about."

"I have a handout from Success Club that you can have, Bob. It gives you more details and verses about this. I'll be glad to answer any questions you have."

"Thanks for all your help, Herb."

"It must be hard to get all this new information at once—well, not new information—it's thousands of years old, but new to you."

"Thanks for understanding how I feel, Herb. It means a lot to me."

"I'm thankful God put us in this room together. We'll share more than the room. We already share friendship, I think."

"Yes, we do, Herb. I'm glad to be your friend. You gave me a lot of things to think about—good things. That's what I need."

*   *   *

Over the next few days, Bob read and re-read the page Herb had given him. It had a lot of verses from Romans on it. Gradually the verses were making sense to Bob, and he began to apply them to his own life.

Herb's testimony of how he accepted Jesus was helping Bob consider the need to connect with Jesus.

If God had provided Herb with the joy of Jesus, maybe God would do the same for him.

Chapter 13

A group of the guys took a hike Saturday afternoon, and Bob was glad to enjoy being outside. There was a huge park—acres of wooded land with trails. It felt good to hear the many birds singing and the red squirrels chattering. That night Bob slept a sound sleep. He was thinking less about prison and appreciating his present life.

Sunday meant going to church. Bob was beginning to feel more comfortable being with the church congregation.

Surprisingly to Bob, the pastor spoke about the "Roman's Road," using the same verses from the book of Romans quoted on the page Herb had given him. He read the first set of verses.

Romans 3:10,23 "...There is none righteous...For all have sinned, and come short of the glory of God..."

The pastor commented on the verse, saying, "God knew that people did bad things long ago and still do bad things today—we think bad thoughts, say bad words, and do bad actions—these are our sins. Nobody is good enough to get into heaven, no matter how obedient we are, how often we go to church, or how many good works we do." The pastor then read the next verse.

Romans 6:23 "For the wages of sin is death; but the gift of God is eternal life through Jesus Christ our Lord."

The pastor explained, "The punishment for sin is to go to

hell; we deserve punishment in hell. God does not want us to go to hell when we die; He wants us to live forever in heaven with Him." Then the pastor read another verse.

Romans 5:8 "**But God commendeth his love toward us, in that, while we were yet sinners, Christ died for us.**"

The pastor said, "God showed His love for us by sending His Son, Jesus Christ, to shed His blood and to die on the cross to pay the punishment for all the bad things we do—to save us from punishment in hell."

The pastor emphasized how God loved everyone so much that He sent His Son, Jesus Christ, to be crucified on the cross to pay for our sins. He quoted John 3:16, the same verse quoted on the back of the success pamphlet.

Bob remembered how the counselor had spoken to him about God's love and had him read verses about God's love.

Then the pastor returned to another passage in the book of Romans and read several more verses.

Romans 10:9-10,13 "**That thou shalt confess with thy mouth the Lord Jesus, and shalt believe in thine heart that God hath raised him from the dead, thou shalt be saved. For with the heart man believeth unto righteousness; and with the mouth confession is made unto salvation…For whosoever shall call upon the name of the Lord shall be saved.**"

The pastor continued on with his explanations. "'Salvation' is Jesus saving us. He came '...to save...' (Luke 19:10)

"Jesus paid for our sins on the cross. 'Who his own self bare our sins in his own body on the tree...' (I Peter 2:24)

"This free payment is a gift we can receive. God made salvation a gift to us; this shows His love for us, and it also keeps us from committing the sin of having pride in our salvation that could happen if we were able to work our way to heaven. 'For by grace are ye saved through faith: and that not of yourselves: it is the gift of God: Not of works, lest any man should boast.' (Ephesians 2:8-9)

"We need to remember not to brag about being saved and be sure to give the credit to Christ, to God. 'But he that glorieth, let him glory in the Lord.' (II Corinthians 10:17)

"We are not SELF righteous. We are CHRIST-righteous. He made the sacrifice for us. He paid for our sins with His life. As I John 1:7 states, '...the blood of Jesus Christ his Son cleanseth us from all sin.'

"Nobody should wait to accept God's Gift—Jesus.

'...now is the accepted time; behold, now is the day of salvation...' (II Corinthians 6:2)

"Note that the verse says **now**, not tomorrow, not sometime in the future. Is today YOUR day of salvation?

"We all like gifts; God offers us His Son, Jesus, the Best Gift; we only have to **repent** our sins, **believe** the gospel message, and **receive** Jesus. '...repent ye, and believe the gospel.' (Mark 16:15)

"Everyone please bow your heads. If you are saved, thank God for His Gift, Jesus, and pray that others will accept

Jesus. If you have not accepted Jesus, use this quiet time to think about it or pray about it. If you would like help in carrying out your decision to accept Jesus, please speak to me after church."

Bob bowed his head and decided to talk to the pastor.

After the closing prayer, Bob nudged Herb and said he wanted to talk to the pastor. Herb assured Bob that the group of men would wait for him.

*　　　*　　　*

"Bob," said the pastor, "how did you come to this decision to accept Jesus today?"

"Your quotations from the Bible made sense to me. I've been hearing verses about salvation at Success Club and Success Workshop and from my roommate. He even gave me a copy of 'Roman's Road' quotations and told me how he accepted Jesus. It all fits together. I realize I've committed many sins and I'm sorry for them and I need Jesus Christ to pay for them."

"I'm glad you've heard many Scriptures about salvation and believe them. Would you like to pray to God and accept Jesus?"

"Yes, but can I read the prayer from the success pamphlet? I'm not used to praying."

"I'm sure God will understand if you use your own words, but if you prefer to use that prayer on the pamphlet, that's O.K., too."

Bob took the pamphlet out of his Bible and read the prayer.

"'Dear God, I agree with Your words in the Bible about salvation. I admit I am a sinner. I am sorry I sinned. I believe that You sent Jesus to die on the cross in payment for my sins. I believe he rose again and lives in heaven. I accept Your Gift of Jesus in payment for my sins and for everlasting life with You, God. Thank You for this Gift.

Please help me to travel to success—to be the person You want me to be. I pray in Jesus' Name, amen.'"

The pastor added his words to the prayer. "God, I thank you for Bob's decision. Please guide him as he starts his new life as a Christian. I pray in Jesus' Name, amen."

Chapter 14

Bob sat in the counselor's office. Jim noticed a change in him. He seemed calmer and he was smiling.

"How was your weekend?"

"It was great."

"Did Herb help you look up the verses on the back of the success pamphlet?"

"He sure did. He also told me how he was saved. He gave me a paper with 'Roman's Road' on it.

"Were the verses meaningful to you?"

"Yes. Then on Sunday, the pastor preached about salvation, and I accepted Jesus as my Savior in the pastor's office."

That brought a smile to the counselor's face. "I'm so happy for you. Remember how, in your first session, God's Word is true and works to bring good results that please God?"

"Yes," answered Bob.

"It was God's Scriptures that led you to Jesus. God must have been so pleased to hear your prayer of accepting Jesus. Welcome to the family of God." Jim stood and shook hands with Bob.

Then Jim sat down and asked Bob, "Did you record the date on the back of your success pamphlet?"

"No, I didn't."

"Will you take a moment and do that now? It would also be good to record the date in the front of your Bible. It's a day to remember—your spiritual birth date."

"I never thought of it that way. Yes, I will take a moment to record the date."

Jim had more to say about Bob's decision. "Now we can really make progress. Accepting Jesus is a prerequisite for success. As you know, be base the counseling here on the Bible and pull things together with the '8 steps to success.'"

"Yes, I've learned the 8 steps."

"I'm not sure if you realize it, but you're already using the 8 steps. You've been reading God's truth in the Bible—step 1. You've accepted Christ as your Savior by praying; step 7 is 'communication,' and prayer is speaking to God. You've done other steps as well. You'll keep learning a lot about success at the Success Club meetings. From now on, the counseling sessions will focus on the sins that landed you in prison—especially the sin of gambling."

"I don't mean to contradict you, but my embezzling is what put me in prison."

"Yes, Bob, but other sins led to that. I record some notes about what we cover during our sessions. I was looking over the notes before you came in, and I noticed that you said the economy got bad, sales dropped on your used car lot, and you began to supplement your income with casino winnings. Why did you do that?"

"To keep my lifestyle as it was before the economy got bad."

"What did you want that the fewer car sales couldn't provide?"

"There were the house payments, car payments."

"Did you give up any luxuries?"

Bob looked down. "No. I used credit cards for new clothes, restaurants, a new TV—other stuff." He looked up with a troubled look in his eyes.

"Hebrews 13:5 states that we should "…be content with such things as ye have…." Were you content?"

Bob hung his head and softly answered, "No."

"I appreciate your honesty, Bob. This is a great start in the right direction. Do you realize that being discontent with what God has provided is a sin?"

"I never thought about it."

"Did you ever stop to think you could get along with less?"

"The thoughts entered my mind, but I sort of ignored them."

"One of the things to be done before you leave Success House is to figure out how to budget. We have a volunteer who comes here occasionally to present a finance program."

"But when I rebuild the business, I won't need to cut back," protested Bob.

"This person will teach you how to use your money in a way pleasing to God."

Bob thought to himself, *What have I gotten myself into by choosing to live at Success House?*

It was as though Jim could read Bob's thoughts. Jim said, "You'll be learning a whole new way of life as you live here at Success House. The changes in your life might seem strange to you at first, but eventually you'll see that God's way will work best for you.

Back at your first counseling session, you blamed your

gambling on the bad economy and crooked politicians. Now you can see that your yearning for luxuries and then buying the luxuries led to gambling. When you read God's truths, you can learn to recognize the lies in your life—step 2 to success, and then you can change and live according to God's truths. You are definitely making progress to success.

Jim paused momentarily to let the truth of his statement sink into Bob's brain. Then he closed by saying,

"I'd like you to memorize the verse I mentioned today. Before we close in prayer, let's look up the verse together and you can underline it in your Bible and write the reference on your bookmark."

Hebrews 13:5 "…be content with such things as ye have…"

Chapter 15

At the beginning of the next counseling session, Jim again reviewed the notes he had written down at the first session.

"During our first session, you said that you decided to supplement your business income with casino winnings. Last week we covered the truth about being content. Did that information make any sense to you?"

"At first it didn't, but, when I thought about it, I realized I wanted more than I had, more than I needed. I had started with a nice home, but then I wanted a newer and bigger and better home, and took out a new mortgage for a new house that I didn't need. I did the same with my car, my clothes, my 'big boys' toys'—a big screen TV, a boat...the list goes on and on. I did this before the economy got bad, so I was already deep in debt before car sales began to decrease."

"Did you ever stop to think that the money you were spending actually belongs to God?"

Bob looked up in surprise.

"Turn to Haggai 2:8. It's in the Old Testament."

Bob turned to the book list at the front of his Bible and found Haggai, noted the page number, and thumbed through his Bible until he found Haggai. He was glad Herb had shown him the book list in the front of the Bible.

"We'll read it together. Then you can underline the verse and mark the Haggai reference on your bookmark."

Haggai 2:8 "The silver is mine, and the gold is mine, saith the Lord of hosts."

"This is probably a new concept for you," remarked Jim.

"It sure is. I always thought that the money I earned was mine. I worked hard for it."

"If you stop and think about God creating the entire world and everything in it, you'll begin to see the bigger picture. God created the gold and silver deposits in the earth. All men did was dig them out and process the minerals. God created the trees from which paper is made, the paper used to print paper money. Viewing the world in this way can be mind-boggling, yet it helps us understand the great power of God, the generosity of God. Let me read you two verses that summarize these truths."

"...by him were all things created..." Colossians 1:16
"Every good gift and every perfect gift is from above..." James 1:17

"If you look at what you have from this perspective, you'll become grateful instead of greedy or selfish or jealous. Now this covers a lot of territory and might be overwhelming at first, but God's wisdom will gradually sink into your mind. God gave you a sound mind, and you'll be making good use of it during these sessions and the hours between sessions. II Timothy 1:7 tells us, 'For God hath not given us the spirit of fear; but of power, and of love, and of a sound mind.' You read this verse now."

Jim gave Bob time to look up the verse and read it.

"Is it O. K. if I underline this verse? It's a good reminder for me to use my brain before I jump into action."

"It's your Bible, Bob," answered Jim. "You don't have to ask me before writing in it."

Bob underlined the verse and noted the reference.

"Between now and the next session, concentrate on Haggai 2:8 until you accept the truth that everything, including money really belongs to God. In addition read Genesis, chapters 1 and 2. Genesis is the first book of the Bible and tells about the beginning of the earth—how God created it and filled it with plants and animals and people."

*   *   *

Walking back to his room, Bob began to think about the truths he had just heard and thought, *God is so amazing!*

Chapter 16

"Let's begin this counseling session with a prayer of thanks to God," said Jim.

Jim bowed his head and closed his eyes. Bob did the same.

Jim began to pray. "Dear God, Heavenly Father, thank You for bringing Bob here to Success House. Thank You for Success House and everything You provide—all that You created. Thank You for Jesus and for Your truths in the Bible. Thank You for sending the Holy Spirit to help us understand Your truths. In Jesus' Name I pray, amen."

Jim and Bob raised their heads and momentarily their eyes locked.

"Have you had enough to think about from the last counseling session?" asked Jim.

"I sure have. As you said, it's beginning to fit together and make sense."

"In one of our earlier sessions, Bob, you said embezzling was what got you into prison. I still maintained that gambling and other sins led to the crime of embezzling. Do you remember that discussion?"

"Yes," confirmed Bob.

"Recently we covered the sin of discontentment that goes along with the sins of materialism, greed, selfishness, and jealousy. Then we looked at the big picture that everything, even money, belongs to God, because He created everything. This time we prayed a prayer of thanks to God."

"I follow what you're saying," commented Bob.

"That's good," said Jim. "Are you beginning to realize that other sins led to the gambling and then the crime of embezzling?"

"I'm gradually seeing that many sins led up to the embezzling."

"Are you realizing that YOU are responsible for these sins, and that you should not blame them on a bad economy or crooked politicians as you did in an earlier counseling session?"

"Yes."

"Have you told God that you're sorry for these sins?" asked Jim.

"At every Success Club meeting, we silently confess our sins. I'm not sure if I confessed all of them."

"God knows what is in your heart, Bob. Are you sorry for your sins?" asked Jim.

"Yes," replied Bob.

"Do you realize that these sins hurt God as well as hurting you and your family and your business?"

"I'm not sure. I usually think of my sins as hurting people," replied Bob.

"I appreciate your honesty. In one of our first counseling session, we read John 9:31 that tells us we have to have a clear conscience—confess our sins—or God won't hear our prayers.

"God sees all our sins. Whether it's day or night, He sees your sins, hears your sinful words; He even knows your sinful thoughts. Psalm 44:21 says that God '...knoweth the secrets of the heart'"

"I guess that means we can't hide our sins from God."

"Yes," agreed Jim, "but beyond that, we have to realize that God not only sees our sins, but is hurt by our sins. John 14:15 says, 'If ye love me, keep my commandments.' Obeying God shows God how much we love Him. Disobeying God shows lack of love for God.

Remember, God sees ALL your sins—day and night, your sinful thoughts, words, and actions."

"I never heard anyone explain things that way," exclaimed Bob in amazement.

"Are you beginning to realize that your sins hurt God?"

"Yes, I am," replied Bob earnestly.

"We'll have a few minutes of silence now. If you want to do so, this would be a good time to tell God you're sorry you hurt Him with your sins and ask Him to forgive you."

"Dear God," prayed Jim silently, "as You know, I'm not used to praying, but I want You to know I am truly sorry for hurting You with my sins. I knew people see my sins and get hurt by them, but I never thought about how You see my sins and that they hurt You. Please forgive me. Please help me to be better for You, dear God." Then Bob remembered how Jim ended his prayers, and Bob added, "In Jesus' Name I pray, amen."

Meanwhile Jim prayed for God's help in the counseling session.

After the silence, Jim saw Bob lift up his head and open his eyes. Jim knew it was time to give Bob some reassurance.

"I assume you confessed your sins to God and asked for His forgiveness. I John 1:9 tells us about God's forgiveness.

'If we confess our sins, he is faithful and just to forgive us our sins, and to cleanse us from all unrighteousness.'"

"I never heard that verse before. I like it."

"So do I," added Jim. "You said you knew your sins hurt people. Have you asked people to forgive you?"

"I've asked my wife to forgive me when I say nasty things."

"Have you asked your wife or any other people to forgive you for gambling and for the sins related to your gambling?"

Bob paused and thought for a moment, then answered, "No, I don't think I have."

"Do you think you should?"

Bob pause and thought again, then replied, "I guess I should, but I don't get to see them anymore."

"Whom did you hurt by your gambling and the sins related to your gambling?"

Bob gave the question some thought. "I hurt my wife and kids. I lost the house and two good cars. I neglected them when I went to casinos." Bob went quiet, thought some more, and continued on. "Of course, I hurt my business partner who is my cousin as well. I stole from the business and almost destroyed the business."

"Do you want these people to visit you?"

"I don't want my kids to see me here. I didn't let them visit at the prison. My wife came to the prison only a few times. I can't blame her for staying away. My business partner doesn't want anything to do with me."

"Would you consider writing each of them a letter asking for their forgiveness?"

"Yes, I think I should."

"You have paper in your desk. Just ask for envelopes and stamps at the main office. I'll send a note over there, so they'll be expecting your request. Are three stamped envelopes enough?"

"No, five would be better. I want to send each of my three children a letter to make it more personal for them—something they can keep for themselves and read it over and over again—if they want to."

"The letters won't guarantee that they'll forgive you, but you will have at least done your part. Be sure the letters say exactly how you have specifically hurt each of them and ask for their forgiveness. Accept the blame for what you did and don't make any excuses. Ephesians 4:15 says that we should be '…speaking the truth in love….' God hates lies and people don't like to be lied to, so be completely honest."

"I'll do my best," promised Bob.

"I'm sure you will. If you want me to proofread the letters stop in and see me whenever I'm free."

"Thank you, Jim."

"You're welcome, Bob. By the way, it will be helpful to pray before you write the letters."

Bob glanced at the clock and stood up.

"Stay a few minutes longer, Bob. I know it's been a long session and we've already run overtime, but I haven't given you the Scriptures to read for next time. My next appointment has cancelled out. Do you have a little more time to spare?"

"Sure, said Bob as he sat down again.

"As you know, most of the counseling sessions from now on will be concentrated on gambling. Let's turn to the book of Proverbs—that's near the middle of the Bible. We'll start in chapter 28."

When both men had found chapter 28, Jim requested of Bob, "Will you please read verses 20 and 22?"

Bob began to read.

Proverbs 28:20,22

"A faithful man shall abound with blessings: but he that maketh haste to be rich shall not be innocent. He that hasteth to be rich hath an evil eye, and considereth not that poverty shall come upon him."

"Bob, take a moment and underline those two verses and mark the references on your bookmark, so you can concentrate on those verses after this session. Then read the underlined verses a few time and think about them between now and the next session."

*   *   *

Bob prayed about the letters and gave them a lot of thought before he wrote them. Then he checked them to be sure he didn't make any excuses or blame others for his sins.

He brought them to the main office of Success House and inserted them in stamped envelopes. The secretary assured him that the letters would be at the post office at the end of the day.

Bob was used to waiting months for mail in prison, but he eagerly awaited replies to the five letters he'd written. He hoped his family would read the letters and believe he was sincerely sorry and forgive him.

Chapter 17

"Bob, at the end of the last counseling session, I gave you two verses in Proverbs to read. I also asked you to think about them—to meditate on them. Back in our first session, we covered Joshua 1:8 that tells us to read God's truths, meditate on them, and apply them. In the same verse, God promises success by doing that—success being God's kind of person. Now, what do you think about those two verses that you read in Proverbs 28?"

"The verses helped me realize I was in a hurry to get money to keep my lifestyle of luxury, and instead I only got poorer."

"This is really true wisdom, Bob. God's words are really entering your mind and heart. Over the next sessions, we'll be going deeper and deeper into the topic of gambling, but, for now, I want you to consider the verses some more. Do you realize you were in a hurry to make extra money?"

"Yes, I do. I wasn't willing to give up luxuries while I waited for car sales to improve."

"That covers the parts of verses 20 and 22 that both mention being hasty to get rich. Will you open your Bible and read those verses in Proverbs 28?"

Bob found the chapter and then saw the underlined verses and began to read.

"'A faithful man shall abound with blessings: but he that maketh haste to be rich shall not be innocent. He that hasteneth to be rich hath an evil eye, and considereth not that poverty shall come upon him.'"

"Now look at verse 20 and note that it mentions not being innocent. Then look as verse 22 that mentions an evil eye.

"I looked up the meaning of 'innocent' in Hebrews, and it refers to being guiltless, blameless. I also looked up the 'evil' in evil eye and I'll read you some of those meaning now." Jim opened a huge book titled, <u>The New Strong's Exhaustive Concordance of the Bible</u>. I'll just read a few of the words—bad, harm, hurt, mischief, misery, sorrow, trouble, wicked, wrong.

"Do you realize that your hurry to get money led to evilness and the misery that goes with sin?"

"Yes, I do. The counseling sessions have guided me to realize how my impatience with a lower income led to my sins—my discontent and unwillingness to adjust to living with less money."

"The end of verse 22 states that those hurrying to get rich don't realize it can result in getting poorer. What happened in your life as you hurried to get rich? In what ways did you get poorer instead of richer?"

"Well, when I had losses at the casino, I first dug into the household money, and we had less food and other household items. Then, without my wife's knowledge, I dug into our kids' college fund, then our savings. I was in charge of the household finances, so, except for the household fun changes, my wife didn't realize what I was doing with the bank accounts. Then I had to have her signature when I put a second mortgage on our house, so I told her it was the bad economy bringing down car sales."

"Didn't she notice you being gone a lot—the time spent at casinos?"

"She knew I was gone more, but she thought I was just working extra hours to improve car sales. Also, I bought a lot of lottery tickets, and it doesn't take much time to do that—just a quick stop at a grocery store or gas station."

"What happened then?"

"Well, we lost the house and had to rent. We had to sell our two good cars and buy an old junker for me to get to work. It was around that time that I began to embezzle from the business—a little here, a little there. It was easy, because I was good at numbers and in charge of the books. As you know, my business partner was also my cousin. We'd known each other since we were kids, and he trusted me. Before this he'd never had a reason not to trust me."

"How did he discover your deceit?"

"The bank notified us that the business was facing bankruptcy, so an auditor was called in to check the books. It didn't take him long to find out how I'd embezzled the company funds."

"Did the business go bankrupt?"

"No. When I was arrested the news hit the newspaper. My cousin went and talked to the bank. He sold his house and cars, hired a bookkeeper, and managed to hold onto the business. He had to work more hours than ever to go to the car auctions and run the business. He wife helped out at the business. She had to give up being a stay-at-home mom."

"What about your wife?"

"She also had to go back to work and leave our kids with neighbors and relatives. She moved into a small apartment and drives the old car. She gets good stamps and shops at thrift stores. She's been great, but I know she's suffering. I think she was hurt most of all by my deceit. She no longer trusts me, and I can't blame her."

"What about the kids?"

"They don't know all the details, but my oldest son is angry. The younger boy is confused. My little girl misses me."

"How did your business partner react?"

"First he blew up in anger and then went silent. He had to testify against me at the trial. I haven't heard from him since I went to prison. I miss his friendship, but I understand some of how he must feel."

"Do those verses in Proverbs make a lot of sense to you now?"

"Yes, they do," said Bob in a sad voice.

"I can see you are truly sorry for how you have hurt those people. Did you write those letters asking for forgiveness?"

"Yes, I did."

"Have you ever forgiven yourself?"

"I blame myself for all of it."

"But have you forgiven yourself?"

"I guess not."

Jim took a moment and printed the word 'FORGIVENESS' on a piece of paper. Then he showed it to Jim and asked him, "What word is in the middle of 'forgiveness'?"

Bob looked and answered, "'Give.'"

"Last week you asked God to forgive you and heard the quotation of I John 1:9 that told how God forgives us when we confess our sins. If God, Who never lies, says He forgives you, can you forgive yourself?"

"But I hurt so many people. I hurt God."

"Yes, you have. You know you also hurt yourself with your sins, but we are supposed to always go God's way. If God forgives, so should we. Ephesians 4:32 states: 'And be ye kind one to another, tenderhearted, forgiving one another, even as God for Christ's sake hath forgiven you.' Luke 10:27 says to '...love the Lord thy God...and thy neighbour as thyself.'

"God is loving and forgiving. He loves you and forgave you. Can you do the same for yourself? Can you love yourself—not in a selfish, self-centered way, but in a healthy way? And can you forgive yourself?

"You don't have to answer that now, but think about it.

"Our time is almost up, so I'll give you the verse for our next session. Look up Ephesians, chapter 4, verse 28.

Jim paused while Bob looked at the book list and found the book of Ephesians, then chapter 4 and verse 28. "Take a moment and underline the verse and put the reference on your bookmark." Meanwhile, Jim looked up the verse in his Bible.

When Jim found the verse, he said, "Let's read the verse together, Bob.

Ephesians 4:28 "Let him that stole steal no more: but rather let him labour, working with his hands the thing which is good, that he may have to give to him that needeth."

Then Jim said, "Take time to read all of chapter 4 before our next session. There is a lot of wisdom there."

<u>Chapter 18</u>

"How did you week go, Bob?" asked Jim.

"It's been busy. Success Club meetings are great. I'm learning a lot about recognizing lies in my life and using God truths in my life."

"Did you think about forgiving yourself?"

"I gave it lots of thought."

"Did you forgive yourself?"

"After struggling about the decision, I decided to forgive myself as God forgives."

"Good. Good."

"Yes," agreed Bob.

"Did you get any answers to the letters you sent?"

"Not yet."

"Well, it hasn't been long since you mailed them. It might take them awhile to write their answer, too. Step 3 to success is repenting of your sins. You've done that well in regard to gambling.

"Meanwhile, it's time to work on step 4 to success. I had asked you to read all of chapter 4 of Ephesians. Did you do that?"

"Yes."

"Turn to that chapter of Ephesians."

Both men opened their Bibles and found the chapter.

"Now, read the verse aloud, Bob."

"'That ye put off concerning the former conversation the old man, which is corrupt according the the deceitful lusts....'"

"Now underline the verse and put a box around the words, 'put off'."

Jim saw Bob box in the two words.

"Read verse 24, please."

"'And that ye put on the new man, which after God is created in righteousness and true holiness.'"

"Now underline the verse and box in the words 'put on.'"

After Bob did this, Jim had him read and underline verse 27.

"'Neither give place to the devil.'"

Jim paused while Bob underlined the verse, and then Jim asked, "Do you have your success pamphlet with you?"

"Yes," replied Bob. "I keep it in my Bible."

"Take it out and read the information for step 4."

"'REPLACE my sinful thoughts, words, and actions with godly thoughts, words, and actions. "…put off…the old man…put on…the new man…Neither give place to the devil." Ephesians 4:22,24,27'"

"As you can see, Bob, those quotations are all from the verses you just read. You're not an 'old man', but the verse was referring to your old sinful self. The new man is the godly person you are now learning to be. Do you know why verse 27 is included in the group of verses for step 4?"

"I'm not sure."

"If you just put off your old ways, you leave an empty space in your life. If you don't fill that space with new ways, you can easily fall for the devil's tempting to return to ungodly ways to fill the empty space in your life."

"Now the verses make sense," exclaimed Bob. I remember

in Success Club we learned that when God gives us a 'don't', He also gives a 'do.'"

"That's right. For example, God says not to lie, but to tell the truth. He tells us not to hate, but to love. He tells us not to hurt, but to help. Now turn to verse 28 in the same chapter and read it aloud. That's the verse you underlined and read at the end of the last session."

"'Let him that stole steal no more: but rather let him labour, working with his hands the thing which is good, that he may have to give to him that needeth.'"

"Bob, what does the verse tell you not to do?"

"Don't steal."

"What does the verse tell you to do?"

"Work with my hands to give to the poor."

"We know you have embezzled, which is a form of stealing. Do you realize that gambling is a form of legalized theft?"

"I don't understand what you mean by that."

"The owners of casinos and many other forms of gambling have ways of getting money that belongs to you and other gamblers."

"Yes, but what about when I won? That wasn't stealing."

"In a way, it was. You were taking what had belonged to other gamblers."

"That's a strange way to look at it."

"Stop and think about it."

Jim stayed quiet for about two minutes, which seemed a long time of total silence, except for the ticking of the clock.

Then Jim spoke out. "It's beginning to make sense. It's

easy to say that gambling owners are stealing. That's probably why the nickname for slot machines is 'one-armed bandits.' Some machines have a handle—like an arm—to pull, and usually the machine keeps the money."

"That's true."

"It's harder to admit that my winning at gambling is a form of stealing from others, but, if I look at it honestly, I can see that it is."

"That's great. You're making good progress for success. Can you see how step 4 fits in?"

"Is that where rebuilding the used car business fits in?"

"No exactly. That's more of a form of restoring—replacing what you took or destroyed. You can build up the business to help restore some of the financial losses that you caused for your business partner and family with your gambling. That is a good thing to do—if your business partner trusts you to be part of the business again.

"However, Ephesians 4:28 says to work with your hands to give to the needy. Now there are all sorts of ways to do this, especially once you leave Success House. While you're here, though, I have a specific plan for you to carry out this verse."

Bob looked hesitant and unsure as he asked, "What is that?"

"Well, gradually you've gained more and more freedom as you have lived here. You can take walks alone, go farther and farther. You can go to stores, the library, and other places. I've spoken to your parole officer and he believes you are now trustworthy enough to work in a store."

"What kind of store?"

"Remember the verse we covered today that said to quit stealing and work with your hands to give to the needy?"

"Yes."

"I'd like you to work as a volunteer at the thrift store near here. Have you ever been there?"

"I've looked around in the store a few times."

"That store takes in donated items—furniture, clothes, and other items. Some of the clothing and furniture is given directly to poor people, but much of it is sold. The profits are used to buy food to stock their food pantry to give to the needy."

"I understand how that works. My wife now has to shop at thrift stores. The food stamps cover her groceries, so she doesn't have to go to a food pantry, but she gets almost all the kids clothing there. She's still wearing the clothes she had before I went to prison, but the kids outgrow their clothes. She also buys small appliances there when ours wear out. Sometimes the kids pick out some toys or books, games, puzzles."

"Do you agree this is a good way to replace the sin of gambling?"

"I sure do."

"You'll be helping to carry things in and out, sort donated items, and stock pantry shelves.

"You'll only be working part-time, because it's important for you to attend the counseling sessions, Success Club meetings, and some of the special things, as when people come in to talk about budgeting and other matters.

"Still, it will be a good experience for you, and you will be helping the needy, as the Bible verse says to do."

"Thank you for setting this up for me. When do I start?"

"Next Monday afternoon, 1-4. You have a flexible schedule there, so you won't miss special events here, especially special speakers who will help prepare you for the outside world. We'll aim for Mondays, Wednesdays, and Fridays, whenever there is no conflict in the schedule."

As Bob got up to leave, Jim said, "Read Psalm 138 for next time."

*   *   *

The days seemed to fly by for Bob since he entered the Success House. Days turned into weeks, and weeks turned into months. Bob enjoyed his work at the thrift store. Every week he learned more at the Success Club meetings and at counseling and at church. He made lots of new friends where he lived, where he worked, and where he attended church.

He was becoming familiar with the Bible. He prayed off and on throughout each day. He put his worries aside and trusted God. He recognized that he was becoming more and more successful, more like the person God wanted him to be.

Chapter 19

"Bob, how do you like your work at the thrift shop?"

"It's a privilege to work there. I'm meeting wonderful people. I feel like I'm accomplishing some good in my life. Also, I think about how I'm helping others as, hundreds of miles from here, others are helping my wife and children.

"At our last session, I asked you to read Psalm 138 for this session. Let's open our Bibles and read that Psalm together."

"I will praise thee with my whole heart: before the
gods will I sing praise unto thee.
I will worship toward thy holy temple, and praise
thy name for thy lovingkindness and for thy truth:
for thou hast magnified thy word above all thy
name.
In the day when I cried thou answeredst me, and
strengthenedst me with strength in my soul.
All the kings of the earth shall praise thee, O Lord,
when they hear the words of thy mouth.
Yea, they shall sing in the ways of the Lord: for
great is the glory of the Lord.
Though the Lord be high, yet hath he respect unto
the lowly: but the proud he knoweth afar off.
Though I walk in the midst of trouble, thou wilt
revive me: thou shalt stretch forth thine hand
against the wrath of mine enemies, and thy right
hand shall save me.
The Lord will perfect that which concerneth me:

thy mercy, O Lord, endureth for ever: for sake not the works of thine own hands."

"What did you think about Psalm 138?"

"It reminded me to praise God for all His love and kindness and His words in the Bible. He continued loving me, even after I committed all those sins against Him."

"That's what I hoped the Psalm would do for you. God's Word works—every time."

"Yes, it does. I'm seeing that more and more. Being here is good for me. I'm glad I decided to be here."

"We're so glad to have you here. Let's take a moment to pray."

The men bowed their heads and closed their eyes, and Jim began to pray.

"Dear God, Thank You for bringing Bob here. Thank You for all the progress he is making. Please help us as we meet together today. In Jesus' Name, amen."

Jim pulled out two copies of the book, Successful Help, by Mary Goloversic. He handed one book to Bob. "As I said before, we're ready to dig deeper into the details in the topic on gambling. Turn to topic #167 in this book."

Both men opened their books to the proper page.

"You see the topic box for topic #167?"

"Yes, I do."

"We've already discussed the verses in the topic box—Proverbs 28:20,22. Now we'll be getting into the specifics. I want you to take this book back to your room when you leave and read the entire topic. During most of the rest of our sessions, we will mainly be discussing the 'Lies of Gambling' and the 'Truths about Gambling.'"

*   *   *

Bob returned to his room, at down at his desk, and looked up topic #167 about gambling. As he read it, he began to recognize that many lies listed were lies that he believed. He had heard the lies told by people he knew and on television gambling commercials. Some of the lies he had told to himself. He was surprised at many of the truths. He had heart some of them before, but had denied them or rejected them. He was amazed at all the Bible verses that stated the truths about gambling.

He read on until he finished reading the entire topic. His mind felt overwhelmed trying to absorb it all at one. Then he realized he could absorb it bit by bit—it did not have to be all learned in one day.

It had taken years for him to learn the lies of gambling, but he knew it would not take years to unlearn the lies, because God would help him.

Chapter 20

"Herb, have you ever read an entire success book?"

"No, not from cover to cover, but my counselor used the book titled, <u>Successful Love</u>, at my counseling sessions. It has several topics on drinking that have helped me a lot. I've also read many of the success topics in Success Club. Sometimes I read topics from the five success books in the library here at Success House. When I get out of here and earning money again, I plan to buy all of the success books."

"Were all the topics about lies and truths?"

"Yes, they were. There are five books in the success series, and they cover 182 topics. As you know, we use them in Success Club."

"Yes, we do. I didn't know there was a topic specifically about gambling. I just finished reading it. I'm amazed at all the lies I have believed."

"So was I," replied Herb. "It took me awhile to learn the lies and truths about alcohol, but, before long, I recognized the lies I had believed and used God's truths to cancel out the lies."

"That's encouraging, Herb. It'll take awhile for it all to sink in, but that's O.K. I still have many months to stay here, so there will be plenty of time for me to absorb it all. It's a good idea you have to buy the success books. I know I'll want to re-read what I've read and share it with others."

"We can use the books at Success Club meetings that we attend after we get home. We can even start a Success Club to help ourselves and others," suggested Herb.

"I never thought about starting a Success Club," said Bob. "It's a good idea. Everything is in the books, so we don't need special training."

"So many people believe lies. The success books help us locate the Scriptures needed to recognize lies. As more and more people discover and apply God's truths, fewer and fewer people will be hurt by lies. There would be less gambling and less of all the other sins that ruin lives," added Herb.

"It's mind-boggling to picture God's truths going further and further—all around the world," added Bob.

"Let's go for a walk and talk more about all the good changes that can happen. I have some money someone sent me. Does a hamburger sound good to you?"

"Sound's great."

"Quite a change from prison food, right, Bob?"

"It sure is. Plus I have you for a friend."

"I'm thankful for our friendship, Bob. I'm glad God put us together."

*   *   *

Jim was sitting at his desk as Bob entered the counseling office and sat down.

"I'll be with you in a moment, Bob. I just have to finish putting down a few notes on the counseling session I just finished."

A few minutes later, Jim looked up and asked, "Did you get to read the entire topic about gambling?"

"Yes, I did. It was a lot to take in at first, but then I realized I didn't have to absorb everything in one day."

"That's right. And when you leave Success House, you will be advised to join a Success Club where you can continue your journey to success. Also, the success books—five main ones in all—are available at bookstores."

"My roommate and I were just talking about this recently."

"There are also children's versions of the success books," added Jim.

"What are they called?"

"Stubby the Stubborn Kitten and Raining Cats and Dogs and Fish. Even adults can enjoy those books."

"I might look them over next time I go to a bookstore. My little girl like cats and dogs."

"Let's turn to the gambling topic now. We'll begin at Section A."

Section A

Lie: Gambling is just a way to have fun—games for people of all ages.

Truth: Games of gambling are games of chance—taking a risk of losing your money to win the money of others, and losing money is not pleasurable, not fun; you seldom see smiles at casinos, gambling card games, etc.—even quarrels can erupt.

Proverbs 21:17 "He that loveth pleasure shall be a poor man…"

"Which part of the topic struck home to you?" asked Jim.

"Well, the verse—Proverbs 23:5—sure applied to me. The riches I had certainly did take wings and fly into the slot machines."

"I figured that verse would hit home for you. Let's read it together again." Both men looked up the verse in their Bibles.

Proverbs 23:5 "Wilt thou set thine eyes upon that which is not? for riches certainly make themselves wings; they fly away as an eagle toward heaven."

"One of the lies mentioned in the topic struck home, too. I didn't stop to think that I taught my children to gamble when I gave them money at the carnival to play games to win prizes. It never occurred to me that those games were a form of gambling."

"Well, it's not too late to set them straight when you return to your hometown."

"I'm so glad my children are still quite young. I still have a few years to teach them before they leave home and go out on their own. I hope they'll listen to me."

"We can plant God's truths in their minds and be a godly example."

"I wish I knew all this sooner."

"Paul in the Bible was a terrible sinner. He even persecuted Christians. Then he became a Christian himself and began to preach God's truths to others. He wrote some wise words in Philippians 3:13-14. I'll read them to you.

"'...this one thing I do, forgetting those things which

are behind, and reaching forth unto those things which are before, I press toward the mark for the prize of the high calling of God in Christ Jesus.'"

That reference says not to dwell on the past, but to concentrate on the present. We also should not try to live in the future. Matthew 6:34 tells us, 'Take therefore no thought for the morrow: for the morrow shall take thought for the things of itself. Sufficient unto the day is the evil thereof.' We cannot change the past, but we can learn from it. We cannot predict the future, but we can plan for it.

"We cannot live three days at a time—yesterday, today, and tomorrow. We can live only one day at a time. We can live the best we can for God in the present. We can please God today."

"Will you tell me those references again? I want to underline them in my Bible right now."

"I sure will." Jim waited while Bob wrote down the references.

Then Jim went on to give Bob his next assignment. "I want you to study the Scripture in Section A box—try to memorize it."

The rest of the session passed quickly. Bob was eager to learn, and Jim was glad to teach him.

Chapter 21

Working at the thrift shop was wonderful. Bob soon realized that he gained as much blessing as he gave.

He enjoyed sorting the donated items and setting them out in the store. Several others from Success House also worked there, as well as volunteers from the community and the paid workers—the cashiers and manager. The workers were friendly with each other and enjoyed their breaks together.

It felt so great to be doing good honest work to help others. It was a bit hard adjusting to an out-of-prison and out-of-halfway house environment, but Bob's co-workers accepted him, even though they knew he was an ex-convict.

Bob also appreciated the friendliness of the shoppers. It was helpful to see people going about their normal activities with no prison guards watching over them.

Most of all, Bob enjoyed fixing food boxes for the needy. Some people looked as though they were not poor and some were shabbily dressed. Bob knew you could be well-dressed and still be broke. It had happened to him, so he had empathy as well as sympathy for the needy. Just seeing the people's joy over the food boxes made Bob happy. He was so glad Success House had required him to do volunteer work.

*   *   *

For weeks on end, Bob awaited for mail delivery, hoping for replies to the letters he had sent asking for forgiveness from those he hurt. Finally he received a large manila envelope with his wife's return address. It was in his wife's handwriting. He felt in a hurry to open it, and yet hesitant.

Carefully Bob opened the envelope and took out four envelopes. The one from his wife was on top. He opened it and scanned it and then read it slowly

The first part of her letter was encouraging. She forgave him. In the second part, she said that she didn't trust him, because of his lies and embezzlement.

Bob knew he didn't blame her for not trusting him. He suddenly became determined. He would work hard and honestly and tell the truth, so she could rebuild her trust in him. She said she was willing to try to mend the marriage together with him. That gave Bob hope. He whispered, "Praise God!"

Then he opened the letter bearing the girlish writing of his daughter. She had dotted the letters "i" with hearts, and that loving gesture brought tears to Bob's eyes. There was no blame in her letter. She just said she loved him, missed him, and could hardly wait to see him again. Bob had to take time out and find tissue to wipe his eyes before he could go on the other letters.

The letter from his youngest son was filled with feelings of sadness. His son has felt abandoned by him. He felt he had lost years of time with his dad. He felt frustrated, not understanding why his dad would commit a crime.

The letter from his oldest son was brief. Bob felt the anger behind the short sentences. He resented the sale of the house. He resented the sale of the good cars, just when he was old enough to get a driver's license. He resented babysitting for his siblings while his mother was at work. He resented doing chores his mother and father would usually do. There was no sign of forgiveness in any of the sentences.

Bob slowly put down his son's letter. He hoped he would be able to eventually rebuild the broken bridge of his relationship with his son. There was so much time he had wasted—time gambling and time in prison—that he could have spent with his children and wife. Bob wanted to return home immediately, but he knew he had to absorb God's wisdom while he was a Success House so he could apply the wisdom when he returned home and pass the wisdom on to his son. He could take his family to church, too, so they could have the joy in Jesus he had found.

The last letter had the bold handwriting of his business partner. He started off saying, "I didn't want to write this letter, but your wife urged me to contact you. I don't trust having you as a business partner, as you already know. I don't trust you to buy the cars at auction or to sell them on the car lot. Of course, I don't trust you to do the account books." He went on to say that Bob could clean up the cars and make the minor repairs needed to put them on the lot. He could keep the lot and office clean. MAYBE—he put in capital letters—Bob would eventually earn his trust.

Bob was glad that his business partner has written him, even though he knew he wasn't forgiven by him. It was a start, at least. He would be given the opportunity to prove he could be trustworthy.

Chapter 22

"Jim," said Bob at the beginning of the next counseling session, "I got four letters from home."

"How did the people react to your request for forgiveness?"

"I'm sure my daughter forgives me and so does my wife, though my wife no longer trusts me, because of the lies I told her. My younger son feels abandoned. My oldest son is angry and unforgiving. My business partner doesn't forgive me or trust me."

"Well, the trust can be rebuilt in time. As the forgiveness, you did your part when you confessed to them and asked you to forgive them. God wants each of us to forgive each other. Ephesians 4:32 tells us to be '…forgiving one another, even as God for Christ's sake hath forgiven you.'

"Forgiving can be difficult, yet, if we don't forgive others, it hurts us—not just the sinner. God warns us to forgive and prevent '…any root of bitterness springing up trouble you….' Forgiveness is a gift to sinners. We already noted that the word 'give' is in forgiveness. Hopefully your oldest son and business partner will forgive you soon, so they will not become bitter or resentful or even revengeful.

"We can pray for them to forgive you—in obedience to God, to please God, not to please you."

"I never thought about all those aspects of forgiveness. You've given me something to think about."

Jim handed a success book to Bob. "Let's turn to Section B of the gambling topic. Both men turned to Section B of the gambling topic.

Section B

> Lie: Gambling will solve my money problems and even
>   some of my other problems.
> Truth: Gambling won't solve your problems and it
>   will cause other problems, so use the Bible
>   to solve your problems—work hard, budget your
>   money to cover your basis needs, and skip your
>   "wants."
> Proverbs 3:5-6 "Trust in the Lord with all thine heart;
>   and lean not unto thine own understanding.
>   In all thy ways acknowledge him, and he shall direct
>   thy paths."

"This topic certainly applies to you and your embezzling, Bob."

"It sure does. I believed every lie in that section. How foolish I was to think that gambling would solve the financial problems facing me and the car lot."

"What about those financial problems? Were they all caused by the economic problems facing our country?" asked Jim.

Bob hung his head. "No. Perhaps some were caused by the economy, but not all of them. I remember in another counseling session how you showed me that my own greed and materialistic ways were a big part of my financial problem. I had gone deep into debt during good financial times. Then when hard times came, I wanted to keep all the luxuries I had when car sales were booming. I wasn't willing to cut back in my personal budget. Instead, I chose to gamble to keep up my high standard of living. I was so stupid."

"You were smart in the ways of the world, but not wise in the ways of God."

"I see the difference now. My worldly wants could not be met by lower car sales, but my basic needs could have been met. But I wasn't willing to let go of my wants."

"I'm so glad you can now discern wants and needs. I know some of this is review for you, but we need to stress the need to get back to basics."

"I'm going to have to teach my children that, too, especially my oldest son. His attitudes are very much like mine, especially when it comes to wanting great cars. He wants a sporty car with four-on-the-floor and dual exhausts. He will have to be content with sharing the older model family sedan."

"It will be hard to convince him, Bob, but he can eventually realize the importance of being content with less. Once he learns that, he can apply it the rest of his life. He's still young. It's good to learn that lesson early in life, before going into debt. This wisdom will provide him with contentment and prevent many problems."

"I wish I'd learned that when I was his age."

"Remember we discussed Paul's perspective of looking backwards? We can look back to learn from our mistakes, but we not dwell on the past. We need to use our time and energy and resources to reach forward, to press on towards godly goals.

"Dwelling on the past is a waste of time, thinking 'I

should have.' Instead think of what you will to today and then do it.

"In James 1:22, the Bible says, 'But be ye doers of the word, and not hearers only, deceiving your own selves.' That's another verse for you to underline in your Bible."

Jim waited while Bob looked up the verse and underlined it.

"Let's go to Section C of the topic."

Section C

Lie: Gambling is a good way to socialize; my friends and
   family expect me to gamble with them.
Truth: God provides godly ways to socialize,
   such at attending church and visiting friends; don't
   gamble to please people—stop gambling to please
   God; gambling with friends and family sets a bad
   example for them and for others..
Hebrews 10:25 "Not forsaking the assembling of ourselves
   together..."

"Was gambling a way for you to socialize?"

"No, it wasn't. I usually went to the casino alone. I just concentrated on the gambling. My family and most of my friends do not gamble. I gave up much of my social life to gamble. I neglected my family and friend to go to the casino."

"It's good that the most of the people you know best do not gamble, or you might have to change your choice of friends.

"Section D of the topic goes along with Section C. Let's turn to that section."

Section D

Lie: Gambling is a good way to fill up my spare time.
Truth: Use the time God gives you to lead others to
    Jesus and teach them God's wisdom.
Colossians 4:5 "Walk in wisdom toward them that are
    without, redeeming the time."

"Some people consider gambling to be a good way to use spare time," commented Jim.

"Yes," agreed Bob. "I know people who do that—especially retirees. I realize now how gambling was a waste of time. Also, I realize that each day is a gift from God, and I shouldn't waste any of the time. While here, I've been spending some of my free time at church services and in the community sharing the gospel message with others. I hand out copies of the success pamphlets when I go for walks, and sometimes people tell me their troubles and ask me for advice."

"You've made many good changes in your life, Bob."

"I plan to stick with my new ways when I go home. Already I know many people there who would like to learn the 8 steps to success. I'm sure some would like to learn more about God and the Bible."

"God's wisdom is meant to be shared," agreed Jim. "God's

wise words in the Bible truly do work wonders. Do you plan to continue going to church when you go home?"

"I've been thinking about that. I intend to visit various churches until I find one that uses Bibles during the services. That way I can keep learning about God and maybe meet some Christian friends."

"It sounds like a good plan, Bob. You'll need plenty of spiritual input to keep you strong as you reconstruct your life.

"For the next few days, study the Scriptures in the boxes of Sections B, C, and D. You can use them yourself and keep them in your mind to share with others."

Chapter 23

"Bob, how are things going with your new roommate?" asked Jim at the next counseling session.

"I really miss Herb, but I know he was happy to go back home. I like my new roommate, and I'm trying to help him as Herb helped me."

"That's great."

"I re-read Section E said Bob.

Section E

Lie: Gambling can have the good purposes of raising money for charities and schools and making more jobs.
Truth: Raise charity funds and make more jobs in honest godly ways.
Colossians 2:3-4 Know God's "…wisdom and knowledge. And this I say, lest any man should beguile you with enticing words."

"That section didn't apply to me a whole lot, because I didn't use the slots to raise money for charity, unless I consider myself the charity. I played the slots to help my income.

"Yet, I do remember buying raffle tickets to support athletic teams and playing Bingo at a club that donated money to help the Scouts. I tried to tell myself I was donating to the state education fund when I bought state lotto tickets.

I sure tried to fool myself, but, deep inside, I knew I was just deceiving myself—but I wouldn't admit it."

"How about Section F, Bob?"

Section F

Lie: It's my money, and I can use it to gamble.
Truth: It's God's money to use wisely in a way pleasing to God.
Haggai 2:8 "The silver is mine, and the gold is mine, saith the Lord of hosts."

"Did you realize that your money really belonged to God when you were gambling, Bob?"

"No, I didn't. I always figured it was my money and I could use it any way I wanted to use it. Realizing that everything— even money—belongs to God gives me a different outlook. I realize now that it's God's money entrusted to me and that God sees how I spend it."

"Let's go on to Section G," said Jim.

Section G

Lie: If I lose, I hurt only myself, not anyone else.
Truth: You hurt God and others and yourself.
Exodus 10:16 "…I have sinned against the Lord your God, and against you."

"Bob, does that Bible verse help you realize that gambling hurts God as well as people?"

"I realized when I went to prison—and even before that when I lost my house—that gambling hurts people, especially my wife and kids, but I hadn't realized it hurt God. He hates sin, and it must have hurt Him to see me spend His money at casinos.

"I've also seen how gambling leads to other crimes, including my embezzling. In prison I met prisoners there who had murdered people to get money to gamble. Some sold illegal drugs to get money to gamble. The murders and drugs hurt the people whom God had created!

"The consequences of the sin of gambling spreads far beyond bingo halls and casinos. It's like throwing a pebble into a pond—the circle of ripples spreads out far beyond the original pebble, far beyond the nickel in the slot machine."

"I Timothy 6:10 ways what you just illustrated with your words—'…the love of money is the root of all evil.' Some people misquote that and say that 'money is the root of all evil.' The coins and papers money are neither good nor bad. It's how we used the that is good or bad.

"You're really taking God's words to heart, Bob. Your godly discernment is improving so fast."

"That's thanks to you, Jim."

"No, Bob. Your insights come from God's wise words—not from me. My counseling and the success books include Scripture quotes. It's God's Words that are working in your life. Give God the thanks and praise and glory. Let's pray and do that now.

"Dear God, Father in heaven, we thank You for Your wise words in the Bible. Thank You for Your guidance. We praise

You for Bob's progress. You deserve the glory, and we give You the glory. In Jesus' Name, amen."

The men raised their heads.

"In the next few days, Bob, I want you to study the Scriptures in the boxes of Sections E, F, and G.

"Before we close this session, I'd like to go over one more Scripture.

"We probably read Isaiah 55:11 before, Bob, but let's read it together now. It reinforces what we just discussed."

Both men opened their Bibles and read aloud.

"So shall my word be that goeth forth out of my mouth: it shall not return unto me void, but it shall accomplish that which I please, and it shall prosper in the thing whereto I sent it."

Chapter 24

Bob entered the counseling room and began to talk to Jim as he sat down. "Section H surprised me."

Section H

> Lie: It's O. K. for me to gamble, because I win more often than I lose.
>
> Truth: Some people to win often, but these people win at the expense of those who lose, and often those that lose are rather poor; when you win at gambling, you are getting your own money plus the money that belonged to other people, and this is greed, and, in a way, it is theft.
>
> Proverbs 17:11 "..he that getteth riches, and not by right, shall leave them in the midst of his days, and at his end shall be a fool."

"It never occurred to me that it was wrong to win at gambling! I was just so excited when I won a jackpot. I never stopped to consider that my winnings came from the losers! I thought about my losses of money, but never thought about the losses of others. Sometimes I'd hear their words of anger or disappointment at losing, but it never effected me emotionally.

"Now I realize winning at gambling is not only recouping my own lost money, but also the money lost by those gambling around me or before me. I've seen people sit at a slot machine for hours and earn very little and, when they leave, the next person hits a big jackpot and gets the money put in the machine by the previous loser. Knowing this takes the feeling of celebration out of winning."

"That's real insight, Bob. God's Word and the Holy Spirit are reaching in and softening your heart."

Bob went on to add, "Winning at gambling is like robbing the poor. It's greed."

"How true, how true," agreed Jim.

The two men had a moment of silence to further consider these insights.

"Step 2 to success is recognizing lies, as you know, Bob. I think you have learned the technique of tracking down deceit."

"Yes, I have. I recognize lies in all sorts of places—some TV commercials, some newspaper ads, some books. I hear the lies of people as they chat while they shop at the thrift store. I remember the lies of the convicts at the prison. More and more I'm catching myself as I tell lies and believe lies."

"I'm so happy for you, Bob. I can see you using all 8 steps to success in your life. You're applying God's Word more and more."

"Section I of the gambling topic is easy to understand now, said Bob.

Section I

> Lie: I have enough money, but I want to be really rich and that is a good goal.
>
> Truth: We should have godly goals, not a goal of getting more and more and more money.
>
> Proverbs 28:20 "...he that maketh haste to be rich shall not be innocent."

Bob continued on, saying, "It isn't money that solves problems. It's applying God's truths to my life.

Getting money should never be a life goal—not a moderate amount of money, not a large amount of money, not even a small amount of money. We need to aim to love people and God, not to love money."

"You've just mentioned God's two greatest commandments. Let's read them together in the Bible. Turn to Matthew 22:37-39."

The men read together.

"Jesus said...Thou shalt love the Lord thy God with all thy heart, and with all thy soul, and with all thy mind.

This is the first and great commandment.

And the second is like unto it, Thou shalt love thy neighbour as thyself."

Jim said, "All the commandments are simplified into those two simple commands—love God and love others as yourself."

"It sounds so simple, yet I have to remind myself every day. I love God and I love people, but for a long time I hated myself for the hurt I had causes with my gambling as well as the consequences of all the other sins I have committed throughout my life.

"I had to forgive myself, so I would not keep wasting time feeling guilty.

"I had to learn to love myself—in an unselfish healthy way—as I loved others. When I gambled, I neglected myself—I would skip many means and miss many hours of sleep. Now I know that was lack of love for myself."

"Have you ever had a problem with self-confidence, Bob?"

"Yes—all my life."

"Did you think that, with more money, you could buy more possessions and become more popular and more self-confident?"

"Yes, that sums it up well."

"That could lead you the wrong way again—maybe not into gambling, but perhaps into people-pleasing.

"People tend to want to be popular, but being popular should not be a goal. Wanting to be popular can lead us in the wrong direction. Sometimes we do what people want us to do—even if it is wrong—just to be liked by them. We shouldn't bend to peer pressure. Jesus said, '...Follow me....' That's in Matthew 9:9 We need to be a <u>God-follower</u>. God wants us to obey Him. When we obey God, we please Him.

"Often people please people to be popular. Often they selfishly please themselves. A verse relating to this is Galatians 1:10 '...do I seek to please men? for if I yet pleased men, I should not be the servant of Christ.' Each person needs to be a <u>God pleaser</u>, not people-pleaser.

"Being popular can lead to prideful confidence in yourself. Not being popular can lead to discouragement and lack of confidence.

"Do you still search for self-confidence?"

"Yes, I do."

"I Timothy 6:17 is related to rich people, but is useful for anyone. It says not to '...trust in uncertain riches, but in the living God.....'

"God wants us to trust Him.

"One verse has especially helped me a lot. It is Psalm 118:8. 'It is better to trust in the Lord than to put confidence in man.' I don't need prideful confidence in myself. All I need is confidence in God.

"I remind myself that I am a child of God, as John 1:12 says. 'But as many as received him, to them gave he power to become the sons of God, even to them that believe on his name.' I remember to be thankful to God for being His child and for all the good things in my life.

"I remind myself to please God, not people.

"When I do these things, I no longer am concerned with self-confidence. It is a worldly way to think. I simply trust God. Instead of thinking I have self-confidence, I give God the credit and call it '<u>God-confidence</u>.'"

"I understand what you are telling me, Jim. I need to change my way of thinking about myself."

"I know you have already changed your way of thinking about gambling, as Section J covers.

Section J

Lie: If I keep trying, I will win, so somehow I'll get the money to gamble—even if I have to steal it.
Truth: It is never right to steal for any purpose—even if you did win with the stolen money and replaced it, stealing is still a sin.
Exodus 20:15 "Thou shalt not steal."

"I sure do understand Section J. Those years in prison daily reminded me of my theft of company funds to pay for my gambling. As was brought out in an earlier session, 'embezzlement' is a fancy word for stealing.

"Even though I understand Section J, it was still helpful to read it. There are so many different ways to stead, even taking from the grocery allowance of the family budget. No matter how small the theft, it is still a sin."

"You are a willing learner, Bob. I think that when you return to your hometown, you will be teaching others more than the 8 steps to success. I believe you will share your newly-found Scriptural wisdom in many ways."

"Well, I had to talk a lot in car sales. Maybe I'll use my talking talent to serve God."

Chapter 25

"Today was the day Bob would see his family. He'd hoped for the reunion for many months, but now it was happening. His wife was driving herself and the children hundreds of miles to visit Bob. She had saved a long time for the money for the gas, meals, and a night at a motel, but she hoped it would be worth the wait and the sacrifice.

Bob paced up and down and around by the main entry door of the Success House. Then he spotted his wife and children coming up the main sidewalk. Bob rushed out the door to greet them.

His daughter ran right up to him. "Daddy! Daddy!" she shouted and gave him a big hug.

Then Bob gently embraced his wife.

He saw his oldest son standing in the background, a sullen look on his face.

Bob reached out to shake his youngest son's hand, but his son kept his hands by his sides and looked down at the sidewalk. He still felt as though his dad had abandoned him.

Bob pulled his hand back. The reunion wasn't going to be easy, but it was a start in the right direction. He hoped his family would see the joy of Jesus in him and see that he was a new person.

*   *   *

"Bob, how was the visit yesterday?" asked Jim.

"It was good—considering all that has happened over the last few years."

"Do you want to talk about it, Bob?"

"Yes, I do. My little girl opened right up and poured out her love to me. She greeted me with a hug and chatted about the trip and school and her friend's new dog. She really made the reunion enjoyable."

"What about your sons?"

"My youngest son is still hurting. He thinks I abandoned him. My older son kept his distance. He's full of anger, and I can understand why. Teen years are hard enough without classmates know your dad is in prison. The embezzlement made headline news—it was no secret in our city. The disgrace, the loss of our home, the need for him to help at home while his mom was out working, plus his own part-time work just to have a little spending money—it all added up to hard times for him."

"Remember, Bob, we can learn by going through hard times. Someday your son might look back on this in a different way and forgive you and grow close again."

"I sure hope so," said Bob.

"How was the reunion with your wife?"

"I could see that she still loves me, but she was afraid to open up much. I think she wants to move slowly, so she won't be hurt again, and that is probably good. We decided to write each other often and get to know each other again.

She has good friends who are Christians, and they are helping her study the Bible and recover emotionally. She's begun to take the children to a small Christian church in our neighborhood. Our oldest son doesn't want to attend, but he goes to please his mother. I hope someday he will go to church to please God. My wife is learning some of the same Scriptures you taught me. I think she's accepted Christ as her Savior. Our shared beliefs should bring us closer together."

"I'm so glad the four of you got together. It was a good start towards rebuilding your relationships."

"Yes, it was, and I'm thankful."

"Our main counseling sessions are almost completed. Then we'll drop to one session a week, covering any topic you choose from the list of 182 success topics."

"It's going to be different, seeing you only once a week. I really depend on talking with you twice a week."

"Yes, it will be different, but you are strong in the Lord now. Remember, you depend on God, not me."

Jim paused and went on. "We'll turn to Section K now."

Section K

> Lie: Gambling is not addictive, so I can quit gambling any time.
> Truth: Gambling can easily become a way of life, a bad habit that is hard to break.
> John 8:34 Jesus said, "…Whosoever committeth sin is the servant of sin."

"Section K is on the addictiveness of gambling, and you're well aware of that."

"I sure am. I thought I'd never get hooked on gambling. How wrong I was. I kept telling myself most of those lies listed in Section K. I convinced myself that I would eventually win big, that I just had to go back to the casino one more time, I just had to buy one more lottery ticket. I told myself I could stop any time without help from anyone. I believed my lies. I don't think I realized I was hooked until I got the warrant for my arrest. Then reality set in fast."

"You definitely understand the addiction of gambling. Let's go on to Section L.

Section L

Lie: I can't stop gambling. Truth: With God's help, I can stop. Matthew 19:26 "…with God all things are possible."

"You've already covered most of Section L. You've accepted Christ as your Savior. You've continued to recognize and confess your sins. You put your trust in God and in His words in the Bible. I noticed your Bible no longer looks new. I'm glad to see you're making good use of it.

"You've studied the Scriptures related to gambling. Do you think you can resist the temptation to gamble when you leave this Success House?"

"Yes, I do. I especially like to remember I John 4:4. '…greater is he that is in you, than he that is in the world.' The Holy Spirit lives in me. I have the joy of Jesus. I have God as my heavenly Father. I just have to keep reminding myself of this and God's promises."

"I have another verse for you. It's God's promise to help

you overcome temptation. Let's open our Bibles and read it together."

I Corinthians 10:13

"There hath no temptation taken you but such as is common to man: but God is faithful, who will not suffer you to be tempted above that ye are able; but will with the temptation also make a way to escape, that ye may be able to bear it."

Jim went on to recommend, "This is verse that should be memorized, so you have it handy in your mind when you are tempted."

Bob agreed, saying, "The more I remember the Scriptures the easier it is to keep my thoughts honest. If I keep my thoughts honest, then my words and actions are likely to be honest."

"Well stated, Bob. God's Words are in your heart and your mind. You trust Him. You know you are valuable to Him, useful to Him. Section M tells us about this."

Section M

Lie: There's no future for me—I've lost everything gambling. Truth: God has a purpose for you—He wants you to do good works. Ephesians 2:10 "For we are his workmanship, created in Christ unto good works..."

"The Scripture quoted in Section M tells us we are created by God—through Christ—to do good works. Are you confident that you can live for the Lord, to go for God?"

"I have confidence that God can and will work in my life. I know I have to do my part—not expect God to do it all. I have to be sure to think before I speak or act. I have to stop and ask myself, 'Is this MY will for me or GOD'S will for me?'"

"That's an excellent question for anyone to ask himself. You are following the example of Jesus, Who was so willing to do God's will, even to die on the cross in obedience to God the Father."

"I've learned to follow Jesus, not people."

"As you know, you will be eventually leaving Success House and return to your hometown. How do you feel about this upcoming change?"

"I'm no longer afraid to start over, because I know God is with me wherever I go. I know I will sometimes fail, I will sometimes sin again, but I know I can confess, be forgiven, and get on God's road again. I won't be perfect, but I can be better, keep improving for God. And I have God's promise of success."

"Let's turn to Joshua 1:8 and read that promise again. God was speaking to Joshua, but God's advice works for us as well as for Joshua.

"This book of the law shall not depart out of thy mouth; but thou shalt meditate therein day and night, that thou mayest observe to do according to all that is written therein: for then thou shalt make thy way prosperous, and then thou shalt have good success."

"Over the next week until we meet again, study the Scriptures in the boxes of Sections K, L, M. As you know, it's God's Word that leads you to success here at Success House and will lead you to success wherever you go for the rest of your life.

"You've come a long ways, Bob. Before we end this session, I'd like to quote something to you—Psalm 1:1-3.

"'Blessed is the man that walketh not in the
counsel of the ungodly, nor standeth in the way
of sinners, nor sitteth in the seat of the scornful.
But his delight is in the law of the Lord; and in his
law doth he meditate day and night.
And he shall be like a tree planted by the rivers of
water, that bringeth forth his fruits he doeth shall
prosper.'

"Bob, I can picture you growing like a willow tree by a river."

"Thank you, Jim," Bob said humbly.

NOTE TO YOU, THE READER:

Topic #167 on "Gambling" is found in the appendix of this book. It is taken from the book, <u>Successful Help</u>. by Mary Goloversic.

It would be wise to read it now.

The last 30+ pages of the topic cover the lies and truths about gambling and are grouped into sections A-M.

APPENDIX

(the page numbers are on the Appendix
at the beginning of the book)

Topic #167 Gambling (from the book),
    Successful Help, by Mary Goloversic

Lies, Truths, and Scriptures about Gambling

Information about the Bible
Information about God
Information about salvation, God's Gift—Jesus
Information about Success and the 8 Steps to Success

Using the 8 Steps to Success to Stop Gambling

Four Questions to Use with Information Boxes A-M

Gambling information—Boxes A-M

Discover and Recover Club (D & R Club)
    for Gambling

Gambling Workshop

"Salvation and Success" pamphlet to copy and give
    to people

THIS IS AN EXCERPT FROM
SUCCESSFUL HELP,

A BOOK BY MARY GOLOVERSIC
Copyright © 1995

Topic # 167   **Gambling**

Lie: Gambling is recreation, only a game.

Truth: Gambling is greed—trying to get rich fast with
someone else's money; it is a sin; stop gambling
and be godly.

Proverbs 28:20,22 "…he that maketh haste to be rich shall
not be innocent.
He that hasteth to be rich hath an evil eye, and
considereth not that poverty shall come upon him."

Gambling is taking a risk in paying money (or some possession) in a situation to get more than you paid.

Some put five cents in a slot machine, some put in a $25 token, some bet thousands on a card game, a dice toss, or a horse race; whatever the amount, it is still gambling.

GAMBLING IS A SIN.

Satan wants us to believe that gambling is a game.
God tells us the truth: gambling is a sin.

"Thou shalt not covet…any thing that is thy
neighbour's." Exodus 20:17
"Thou shalt not steal." Exodus 20:15

Gambling is just that—wanting more than is rightfully yours (coveting) and trying to take what is not rightfully yours (stealing).

Gambling is trying to keep your money and take someone else's, too; this is greed.

Gambling is a scheme to get rich quick in an ungodly way.

"...he that maketh haste to be rich shall not be innocent." Proverbs 28:20

Whether you win or lose, gambling is not the wise use of the money God gives you.

If you win, others lose God's money.

If you lose, you lose God's money.

Gambling wastes valuable time God gives us as well as money that God gives us.

"Walk in wisdom toward them that are without, redeeming the time." Colossians 4:5

"The silver is mine, and the gold is mine, saith the Lord of hosts." Haggai 2:8

GAMBLING CAN LEAD TO OTHER SINS.

Neglect of buying basic needs and paying bills/debts

Neglect of eating, sleeping, and increase in severity of stress-related health problems, as ulcers and high blood pressure

Americans were spending more money on gambling than on food at the beginning of the new millennium.

Neglect of yourself, family, friends, and God

Being a poor role model for others

Neglect of occupation and other priorities

Use of "good luck" charms, as "lucky penny," "lucky rabbit's foot"

Loss of what God has provided, as car and house

Theft and murder and more—even suicide from depression over losses

GAMBLING COMES IN MANY FORMS.

Gambling can start even before a person is a teen; it can begin when a child plays chance games at school events or carnivals, bets on a school ball game, plays marbles "for keeps," buys a ticket for a cake walk, pays money to fish in a "fishpond full of little toys, puts money in a machine in hopes of getting a toy, pinball gambling.

Public gambling is open to all adults, as in bingo halls, casinos, racetracks (race horses, dogs, cars, etc.), riverboats, and in other places, such as grocery stores that sell lottery/lotto ticket, gas station with slot machines, restaurants with gambling machines.

Private gambling can take place in home with gambling card games and dice games, at work in ball game point pools, in recreation rooms where bets are made on pool games; sometimes this type of gambling includes teens and children. Gambling can be done on the Internet with casino games, poker, and some types of day trading.

> Note: Casino-type computer games played for fun
> with no real money involved can be an enticement

and temptation to participate in real gambling.

Camouflaged forms of gambling operate for good causes—supposedly, such as a lottery to help support a state education program, bingo for church, raffles and 50-50 drawings to raise funds for charity or church, "Las Vegas nights" to raise funds for organizations, taking unreasonable risks on the stock market and money-making schemes, chain letters related to gaining money.

There is no righteous reason to gamble.

Money can be raised in honest godly ways.

God does not even want an offering composed of gambling profits.

> "For I the Lord love judgment, I hate
> robbery for burnt offering..." Isaiah 61:8
>> This refers to burnt animal sacrifices,
>> but the meaning is there for the
>> offering of any money gotten in an
>> ungodly way.

GAMBLING HAS NEGATIVE RESULTS, EVEN IF YOU WIN.

Gambling is based on the love of money and leads to evil and hurts.

> "For the love of money is the root of all evil: which while some coveted after, they have erred from the faith, and pierced themselves through with many sorrows." I Timothy 6:10
>> Note: The verse says "the love of money is

the root of all evil;" the money itself—the
coins and paper money—is not evil.
"But they that will be rich fall into temptation and a
snare, and into many foolish and hurtful lusts,
which drown men in destruction and perdition."

I Timothy 6:9
"I the Lord search the heart...give every man
according to his ways...
As the partridge sitteth on eggs, and hatcheth them
not; so he that getteth riches, and not by right, shall
leave them in the midst of his days, and at his end
shall be a fool." Jeremiah 17:10-11

GAMBLERS CAN LOSE A LOT OF MONEY AND MATERIAL POSSIONS AND MORE.

Centuries ago Solomon knew greed led to detrimental results.
"The thoughts of the diligent tend only to
plenteousness; but of every one that is hasty only to
want." Proverbs 21:5
"Wealth gotten by vanity shall be diminished..."
Proverbs 13:11
"...riches certainly make themselves wings: they
fly away as an eagle toward heaven." Proverbs 23:5
"He that is greedy of gain troubleth his own
house..." Proverbs 15:27
"He that trusteth in his riches shall fall..." Proverbs
11:28

Today we see how the greed for more money by gambling has detrimental results—to the gambler AND to those around him/her.

Gambling sometimes places you in a environment conducive to hurtful habits, as smoking (or breathing second-hand smoke), drinking, alcohol, sexual immorality, music with evil lustful lyrics. Gambling can trap a person into the gambling habit—a desire to recoup losses, a lust for more wins; it can be addictive; some people are compulsive gamblers.

"He that loveth silver shall not be satisfied with silver; nor he that loveth abundance with increase..." Ecclesiastes 5:10

"Hell and destruction are never full; so the eyes of man are never satisfies." Proverbs 27:20

Gambling can lead to material losses, as loss of jewelry, house, car.

Sometimes homes are lost in one gambling excursion, even on a single bet.

Often pawn shops are located near casinos.

Gambling can lead to monetary losses, such as savings accounts, bonds, stocks, job income (and job loss), and can even end in maxed-out charge cards, bankruptcy, and dire poverty.

Gambling can lead to social/family/relationship losses, such as missing out on the joy of parenting by leaving babies and children alone in hotel rooms or with babysitters while parents gamble, losing friends because of neglecting them, separating of spouses and divorcing.

Gambling can lead to lies and to crime to support the gambling habit—theft (including embezzlement), dealing in drugs, even murder and loss of freedom with prison sentences; sometimes people kill people to pay off their gambling debts and sometimes people kill people owing them gambling debts that they cannot or will not pay.

GAMBLING CAN BE STRESSFUL.

Losing and waiting to win can be stressful

There is stress in waiting in suspense in hope of winning.

There is stress missing a bingo by just one number not called, stress from not placing a bet that would have won, and stress for not playing a few minutes longer at a slot or machine that paid out shortly after you left it.

There is stress and guilt over money lost.

There is pressure to recoup losses.

Though gamblers keep gambling with high expectations, you can sometimes see from the expressions on their faces that many are not enjoying themselves.

Some are bored.

Some are losing hope.

Some are nervous and tense.

Some are worried.

Some are fearful.

Some are depressed.

Some are full of frowns and anger and rage.

Some are worn out from lengthy attempts to recoup their losses before leaving.

Some, especially the card players, probably have an expressionless look of neutrality, "a poker face."

GAMBLERS CAN MISS OUT ON MANY SPIRITUAL BLESSINGS.

At the cross of crucifixion, the soldiers used chance to determine who would get Christ's clothes after He died: instead of being sad about the crucifixion and accepting Christ as their Savior, they were eager to have personal gain.

"Then the soldiers, when they had crucified Jesus, took his garments, and made four parts, to every soldier a part; and also his coat: now the coat was without seam, woven from the top throughout. They said therefore among themselves, Let us not rend it, but cast lots for it, whose it shall be..."
John 19:23-24

One soldier won Christ's coat, but apparently didn't accept Christ as his Savior—the best Treasure of all.

Today, for many people, games of chance are still more important to them than Christ is.

114

They put their time and money and faith in gambling instead of in Christ.

"For what is a man profited, if he shall gain the whole world, and lose his own soul? Or what shall a man give in exchange for his soul?" Matthew 16:16

GAMBLING IS A PROFIT-MAKING INDUSTRY, NOT A GAME OR A MONEY-MAKER FOR MOST GAMBLERS.

The average gambler is willing put his honestly-earned money into gambling, but skilled gamblers, professional gamblers, and the gambling industry often take the money deceitfully.

Sometimes skilled gamblers who know how to count cards or mathematically figure out the odds are not allowed to gamble in some places, because the gambling owners would not make a profit on them; sometimes they are permitted to gamble for a while, but then are asked/forced to leave.

The gambling industry is not based on chance, but is well-researched and designed to show profit for the gambling industry.

Machines and games are researched and designed to attract and hold the attention of the gambler.

The senses are considered in design—

seeing, hearing, feeling, smelling, tasting,

For example, choice of colors is important—green (symbolizing money) and silver and gold (symbolizing wealth) are colors often used on lottery tickets; eye-catching pictures are used on slot machines. Other examples are the bells ringing for jackpots and announcements of winners and more opportunities to gamble; sometimes music is played, perhaps subliminal messages, such as "Keep gambling," "You'll win soon," are inserted into the "canned music."

Mathematical and computer experts, electrical/ electronic engineering specialists, artists and audio people combine their skills to design new games and machines that will entice and entrap gamblers.

For example, there are progressive slot machines.

These inventions can cost hundreds of thousands of dollars, even millions.

Would businessmen invest in such inventions unless a profit was likely?

Of course not.

Who profits from these investments?

The owners/investors profit, not the average gambler.

What are YOUR odds of winning a large jackpot?

The author has heard it stated that, scientifically calculated, you are

more likely to be struck by lightning
(which seldom occurs) than to win a
big jackpot.

Where does the gambling industry get its huge profits?

Losing gamblers provide the profits.

Thousands, even millions, of dollars are spend on advertising on television and radio, in newspapers and magazines, on billboards and posters.

Be careful, "…lest any man should beguile you
with enticing words." Colossians 2:4
"…they that will be rich fall…a snare…"
I Timothy 6:9
"Be sober, be vigilant; because your adversary the
devil, as a roaring lion, walketh about, seeking
whom he may devour…" I Peter 5:8

Thousands, even millions, are spend on enticing you to go to casinos—ways to attract your eyes, ears, nose, taste buds, and sense of touch.

Inexpensive or free plane or bus rides are offered,
free shuttle service to casinos.
There are neon lights and moving lights.
In addition, thousands, even millions, of dollars are
given away—roles of quarters, piles of chips, etc.—
to encourage you to enter the gambling facility.
Casinos often have extravagant décor, like
pyramids, castles, statues, ships, manmade
waterfalls, thick rugs, fountains, and flowers some
even have attractions for children and family fun.
Inexpensive hotel rooms are available with

comfortable beds and soft sofas; "high rollers"—big gamblers—are offered luxurious hotel suites.

Food and drinks are sometimes inexpensive or free. There are often bands/orchestras, singers, dancers, comedians, all sorts of entertainers and shows, even services of prostitutes.

All of these attractions dazzle the eyes, ears, nose, taste buds, and sense of touch, but beware.

"Eat thou not the bread of him that hath an evil eye, neither desire thou his dainty meats:

...Eat and drink, saith he to thee; but his heart is not with thee." Proverbs 23:6-7

"Let no man deceive you by any means..."

II Thessalonians 2:3

Comfort is also important.

Many modern machines simply have computer buttons to push and stools on which to perch to prevent fatigue.

Some games, as bingo, are played at tables and chairs, which is less-tiring than standing.

The monotonous sounds of coins clinking into the machines and the hum of electronic game sounds are almost hypnotic.

One item you probably won't find in a casino is a clock.

Casino owners don't want gamblers to leave.

With bright lights inside and outside the casino, it seems like daytime twenty-four hours a day, helping a gambler lose track of time and keep gambling.

Also, the gamblers watches might be in a local pawn shop.

Everything about the gambling industry tempts people to gamble and tries to keep them gambling.

GAMBLING IS ALMOST A FORM OF LEGALIZED THEFT.

Slot machines with long handles to pull have been nicknamed "one-armed bandits" and some have been designed to look like a robber holding up the prospective gambler; this is an accurate symbol of theft.

Gambling often attracts low-income people (the poor, the young, the retired who can be most easily hurt by it; gambling steals from the poor gamblers and gives to the rich owners of the gambling industry.

"Rob not the poor, because he is poor…" Proverbs 22:22

"He that oppresses the poor to increase riches, and he that giveth to the rich, shall surely come to want." Proverbs 22:16

For every single person that wins a jackpot of millions of dollars, there are thousands and thousands of people who lose, and a gambling industry that gains.

Even millionaires can lose all their money by gambling if they gamble for high stakes or even if they gamble frequently for low stakes or for many years.

Gambling produces one big winner and many losers.

The gambling industry is the big winner.

The gamblers are the losers—big losers and small losers.

WHOM DO YOU BLAME FOR THE SIN OF <u>YOUR</u> GAMBLING?

If you are a gambler, realize that the gambling industry is not to be solely blamed for your losses.

The gambling industry can entice you, but it is YOU, yourself, who yields to the temptation to gamble.

It is YOU who chooses to gamble, YOU who goes to the casino, YOU who put the money in the slot, or buys the bingo cards, YOU who puts the chips on the table.

"…every man is tempted when he is drawn away of his own lust, and enticed.

But when lust hath conceived, it bringeth for the sin…" James 1:14-15

EACH PERSON INVOLVED IN GAMBLING IS RESPONSIBLE FOR HER/HIS PART IN THE SIN OF GAMBLING.

Whom does this include?

Those who sponsor it

Those who accept its profits

Those who design, manufacture, and sell the gambling equipment and supplies

Those who own the place of gambling

Those who sing and dance and cook and clean and guard casinos

Those who sell the "games" at the place of

gambling

Those who run the "games"

Those who play the "games"

God doesn't want you to gamble yourself, and God doesn't want you to work in the gambling industry.

For example, don't be a card dealer in a casino or a seller of lottery tickets in a grocery store.

Don't participate in gambling for any reason, as calling bingo numbers at a fund-raising bingo game (non-gambling bingo is not sinful, but people have to be cautious not to transfer to playing bingo for money).

ARE <u>YOU</u> A GAMBLER?

Do you pay money for the possibility of winning something? If so, you are a gambler.

WHY SHOULD YOU STOP GAMBLING?

You should <u>not</u> stop gambling because of the world's consequences of gambling, such as the divorce caused by gambling, loss of a house by gambling, debt or theft related to gambling, or any other worldly reason.

<u>You should stop gambling to please God.</u>

"…do I seek to please men? for if I yet pleased men, I should not be the servant of Christ."

Galatians 1:10

"And whatsoever ye do, do it heartily, as to the

Lord, and not unto men." Colossians 3:23

As a result, you will have peace, God will listen to your prayers, and you will have godly benefits.

"...the face of the Lord is against them that do evil." I Peter 3:12

"...the eyes of the Lord are over the righteous, and his ears are open unto their prayers." I Peter 3:12

"A good name is rather to be chosen than riches, and loving favour rather than silver and gold." Proverbs 22:1

"There is that maketh himself rich, yet hath nothing: there is that maketh himself poor, yet hath great riches." Proverbs 13:7

Don't just admit the sin; quit the sin of gambling.

"Be not wise in thine own eyes: fear the Lord, and depart from evil." Proverbs 3:7

"...sin no more." John 8:11

EACH GAMBLER NEEDS TO FOLLOW GOD'S WAYS.

<u>Gamblers need to give up their greed for gain.</u>

"...be content with such things as ye have..." Hebrews 13:5

"And having food and raiment let us be therewith content." I Timothy 6:8

Note: The verse on desiring to get rich (verse 9) and the verse on the evil related to the love of money (verse 10) follow verse 8 quoted above.

Gamblers need to trust in God, not in their gambling "luck."

"But my God shall supply all your need according to his riches in glory by Christ Jesus." Philippians 4:19

"In thee, O Lord, do I put my trust: let me never be put to confusion." Psalm 71:1

"Trust in the Lord with all thine heart; and lean not unto thine own understanding.

In all thy ways acknowledge him, and he shall direct thy paths." Proverbs 3:6-7

"Is any thing too hard for the Lord?..." Genesis 18:14

"For with God nothing shall be impossible." Luke 1:37

"...with God all things are possible." Mark 10:27

Gamblers need to work for their income.

People that work to increase their income will receive increase, not just a possibility of gain from gambling.

"...he that gathereth by labour shall increase." Proverbs 13:11

Gamblers need to aim for godly prizes instead of gambling prizes.

"Know ye not that they which run in a race run all, but one receiveth the prize?...

...Now they do it to obtain a corruptible crown; but we an incorruptible." I Corinthians 9:24-25

"I press towards the mark for the prize of the high calling of God in Christ Jesus." Philippians 3:14

"…he that winneth souls is wise." Proverbs 11:30

Note:

Gambling can begin in a non-sinful way, such as getting prizes winning a free bingo game at school, church, or activities center.

Playing bingo or another game can then go to playing for small stakes, as playing bingo by buying bingo cards for a penny each at a community center or retirement home; children might stake marbles in a game of marbles, people might bet a quarter on a school ball game, or someone might spend a half dollar on a carnival game to win a stuffed animal.

However, gambling is addictive with prizes as a goal and providing the thrills of risk, a chance of gain, escape for a problem, outlet for anger, temporary prestige at awarding of prizes, a false way to fight the fear of failure, even a replacement for lost love or a substitute for another addiction. It is best to have godly goals from the start, not worldly goals, such as prizes.

Gamblers need to have Christ as their Savior

If you aren't saved, accept Jesus; He is a free Gift, not a gamble, but a lasting Gift, not something you can lose.

> "For God so loved the world, that he gave his only begotten Son, that whosoever
> believeth in him should not perish, but have everlasting life." John 3:16

"...him that cometh to me I will in no wise cast out."
John 6:37
Jesus will help you battle the desire to gamble.
"I can do all things through Christ which
strengtheneth me." Philippians 4:13

<u>Gamblers can help each other stop gambling; non-gamblers
can also help gamblers stop gambling.</u>
Joining a Success Club.
Join a support group; Gamblers Anonymous has
helped many gamblers.
If needed, seek godly counseling.

LIES LEAD TO GAMBLING.

The act of gambling begins in the brain—with the lies we tell
ourselves, the lies our associates tell us, the lies of advertising.
Gambling is not a game or a secure way to increase your
income, but it is a sure way to lose your money and more
than your money.
The truth is that gambling is a sin—it is a waste of the money
God gives you, and, even if you win, it takes the money of
others.

USING THE 8 STEPS TO SUCCESS IS ONE WAY TO USE GOD'S WORDS TO STOP GAMBLING.

Step 1: Read the Bible
Look for the Bible quotations in these lists that combat any
of the gambling lies you believe.

125

"Search the scriptures..." John 5:39

"And ye shall know the truth, and the truth will make you free." John 8:32

Step 2: Recognize lies

Look over these lies at the end of this topic and carefully and search for the lie that you believe that most influences you; be honest with yourself as you do this self-check

"...let a man examine himself..." I Corinthians 11:28

"Let no man deceive himself..." I Corinthians 3:18

"Let no man deceive you..." II Thessalonians 2:3

Step 3: Repent

Repent of the sin of gambling based on the gambling lie you believed to get out of the gambling trap—admit the sin of gambling and be sorry for it and confess it to God to be free from the guilt of the sin of gambling.

"...repentance to the acknowledging of the truth; ...that they may recover themselves out of the snare of the devil..." II Timothy 2:25-26

"If we confess our sins, he is faithful and just to forgive us our sins, and to cleanse us from all unrighteousness." I John 1:9

"The Lord is nigh unto them that are of a broken heart; and saveth such as be of a contrite heart." Psalm 34:18

Step 4: Replace

Replacement is also part of the plan to stop gambling.

Each gambler needs to turn from gambling and turn to God; they need to replace the sin of gambling with God's good ways, perhaps a special kind of good work for God, such as volunteering to help at a charity thrift store.

I Timothy 6:11 gives some suggestions; we are to flee the love of money and other such sins "…and follow after righteousness, godliness, faith, love, patience, meekness."

Step 5: Love

Accept God's love and brotherly love from others, love God and people, love yourself in a healthy, not self-centered way.

Step 6: Forgive

Forgive others and forgive yourself, ask for forgiveness from God and from people, accept the gift of forgiveness from God and from people, including yourself.

Step 7: Communicate

Communicate with God—talking in prayer and listening in the Bible, communicate with others in an honest loving way—talk, listen, and respond), communicate with yourself in an honest loving way.

Step 8: Help

Ask for and accept help from God and from people, help God, others, and yourself.

CAUTIONS ON STOPPING <u>YOUR</u> GAMBLING.

Don't dwell on your past mistakes or worry about the future, but concentrate on solving today's problems—one day at a time with Jesus.

Do not go near gambling places again; stop close association with any of your gambling partners.

Look for the lies of gambling in your life every day.

Be prepared with God truths to overcome temptation to gamble.

> Memorize **I Corinthians 10:13.**
> **"There hath no temptation taken you**
> **but such as is common to man:**
> **but God is faithful,**
> **who will not suffer you to be tempted**
> **above that ye are able;**
> **but will with the temptation**
> **also make a way to escape,**
> **that ye may be able to bear it."**
> Memorize a specific verse to combat whatever
> gambling lie affects you the most.

GAMBLING CAN BE STOPPED.

If you are the only person in the world to stop gambling, that's at least a little less money in the jackpot to tempt other to use God's money unwisely by gambling.

If every Christian gambler stopped gambling, there would be a lot less money in the jackpot to tempt other, plus many more godly role models in the battle against gambling.

LOOK AT THE LIST OF LIES AND TRUTHS ABOUT GAMBLING.

Read the following list of lies and truths of gambling, even is you are not a gambler.

As you read the lies, keep remembering God's truths, including the following verse:

"…riches certainly make themselves wings; they fly away…" Proverbs 23:5

Lies, truths, Scriptures about gambling, page 1

LIES, TRUTHS, AND SCRIPTURES ABOUT GAMBLING

(This is the last part of success topic # 167 about gambling.)

Section A

Lie: Gambling is just a way to have fun—games for people of all ages.

Truth: Games of gambling are games of chance—taking a risk of losing your money to win the money of others, and losing money is not pleasurable, not fun; you seldom see smiles at casinos, gambling card games, etc.—even quarrels can erupt.

Proverbs 21:17 "He that loveth pleasure shall be a poor man…"

"I said in mine heart, Go to now, I will prove thee with mirth, therefore enjoy pleasure: and, behold, this also is vanity." Ecclesiastes 2:1

"And I will say to my soul, Soul, thou hast much goods laid up for many years; take thine ease, eat, drink, and be merry." Luke 12:19

Some people choose to "..enjoy the pleasures of sin for a season….." Hebrews 11:25

"…lovers of pleasures more than lovers of God…" II Timothy 3:4

"…choked with cares and riches and pleasures of this life, and bring no fruit to perfection." Luke 8:14

"Wilt thou set thine eyes upon that which is not? For riches certainly make themselves wings; they fly away as an eagle toward heaven." Proverbs 23:5

"Eat thou not the bread of him that hath an evil eye, neither desire thou his dainty meats:

For as he thinketh in his heart, so is he: Eat and drink, saith he to thee; but his heart is not with thee." Proverbs 23: 6-7

Lies	Truths
It's only a game; it's only fun, recreation.	In gambling, you pay to play for gain; in other games, you play for fun. (For example, A game like Bingo is not bad, but to play it for profit is wrong.
I just set this amount of gambling funds aside for	Gambling is still a paid game of chance, even if you have fun.
It's only a quarter to play, and my daughter has fun picking up the duck, so She might get a prize. It's only fifty cents and my son had fun trying to knock down the wood bottles with A baseball to try to win a prize. It's fun for kids to pop balloons with darts, and its only seventy-five cents for three tries with the darts to	We need to teach children God's way when they are young, so they will know which way to take as adults.

win a prize.
It's only a dime, and she
might win a whole cake in
the cake walk.
It's fun to try to get the
hoop on a pop bottle, and
it's only a dollar for three
hoops to try to win a big
bottle of pop.

I give my sister money to play bingo.	Don't support the sins of others.
It's fun to bet on my favorite race horse, greyhound dog, race car.	It's fun to watch races without betting.
I only use the coins in my pocket to play; I have a plan and I limit myself.	Any amount is gambling.
Gambling relaxes me; it's pleasurable.	Gambling is stressful and can even lead to insomnia, emotional disorders, and suicide; look at the gamblers around you—not many are likely to look relaxes; many look serious, strained, tense, stressed out, and you seldom see a smile or hear a laugh; some drink while they gamble to relieve the stress.
I like the feel of power I get when I toss the dice or make a bet.	You are under the power of the person who set up the game, and, when you lose, you are likely to feel powerless and depressed.

We planned this gambling trip a long time ago; we get cheap airline tickets, inexpensive hotel rooms at a glamorous resort, low-cost meals and drinks; it's a fantastic deal.	The vacation packages are fabulous to entice you to casinos to gamble; change your vacation plans and budget your trip accordingly; it's better to break reservations at a loss than to be tempted to gamble by staying at a casino resort.
Betting on ballgames makes ballgames on television more interesting.	Ballgames can be enjoyed without betting.
It's the sports pool at work, so I don't want to let the guys down and ruin their fun.	Go God's way—don't let God down; it's better to disappoint people than to disappoint God.
I only flipped a coin and bet on the desserts in my lunch pail and my partner's lunch pail.	Any gambling is a sin.
Other people do worse things than gamble.	Compare your behavior with God's standards, not the behavior of other people.

Section B

> Lie: Gambling will solve my money problems and even some of my other problems.
>
> Truth: Gambling won't solve you problems, and will cause other problems, so use the Bible to solve your problems—work hard, budget your money to cover your basis needs, and skip your "wants."
>
> Proverbs 3:5-6 "Trust in the Lord with all thine heart; and lean not unto thine own understanding. In all thy ways acknowledge him, and he shall direct thy paths."

"Be not wise in thine own eyes: fear the Lord, and depart from evil." Proverbs 3:7

"O Lord, correct me..." Jeremiah 10:23

"For whom the Lord loveth he correcteth..." Proverbs 3:12

"When wisdom entereth into thine heart, and knowledge is pleasant unto thy soul:

Discretion shall preserve thee, understanding shall keep thee..." Proverbs 2:10-11

"Wealth gotten by vanity shall be diminished: but he that gathereth by labour shall increase." Proverbs 13:11

"But my God shall supply all your need according to his riches in glory by Christ Jesus." Philippians 4:19

"And having food and raiment let us be therewith content." I Timothy 6:8

Lies	Truths
I have to gamble because I need money.	Trust God to supply all your needs (not luxuries) or to provide a job for you; pray for provisions. (Read Matthew 6:25-34.) Shorten your "Want List, revise your budget, seek cheaper housing, cheaper clothing, cheaper cars, sell what you don't need. Work longer hours; take a second job. Ask the businesses and people and to whom you owe debts if they would accept smaller payments.
I only have part-time work low pay and need more money, so I have to gamble.	You'll likely end up with less money or no money at all if you gamble; don't risk the little money you do have. Put up ads at grocery stores and offer to use any skills you have, such as sewing, typing, carpentry; check at a senior citizen's centers for odd jobs, such as housecleaning, cooking, cutting grass.
I'm retired and need more money for medicine.	Some doctors have sample pills or access to discounted medicines.
I'm a single mom and need more money to buy food and clothes for my kids.	Some thrift shops give food and clothing to the needy and help with the rent and utilities; some churches also do this.

Gambling is a way to add to my income.	Gambling takes more from Gamblers than it gives back; the casino owners and Bingo hall owners and the gambling machine owners make the profit; for OWNERS gambling is a high-profit enterprise, but for PLAYERS gambling is a high risk; otherwise, the gambling industry would go out of business.
Gambling helps people pay their bills.	Gamblers often neglect their jobs, use their bill payment money to gamble; some lose their homes, some end up filing bankruptcy or out of work or in prison with their reputation destroyed by theft and other crimes committed to get money to gamble.
I need to gamble to pay my gambling debts.	Sometimes people even have lives threatened over their gambling debts. Don't risk going deeper into debt by gambling to pay off gambling debts. Work overtime, sell your excess belongings, use other honest ways to pay your debts.
I've felt guilty since I lost money at gambling, so I'll try to win back my losses to get a clear conscience.	Confess the sin of gambling to God and be free of guilt; don't gamble again.

I quarreled with my friend, so I went to the casino to calm down.	Settle any quarrels as soon as possible.
I escape from my problems when I gamble.	Face your problems and solve them; avoiding problems won't make them disappear, and gambling will probably multiply your problems.

Section C

> Lie: Gambling is a good way to socialize; my friends and family expect me to gamble with them.
>
> Truth: God provides godly ways to socialize, such at attending church and visiting friends; don't gamble to please people—stop gambling to please God; gambling with friends and family sets a bad example for them and for others..
>
> Hebrews 10:25 "Not forsaking the assembling of ourselves together…"

"…as many as received him, to them gave he the power to become the sons of God, even to them that believe on his name…" John 1:12

"A man that hath friends must shew himself friendly…" Proverbs 18:24

"And whatsoever ye do, do it heartily, as to the Lord, and not unto men…" Colossians 3:23

"…do I seek to please men? for if I yet pleased men, I should not be the servant of Christ." Galatians 1:10

"...neither be partaker of other men's sins: keep thyself pure."
I Timothy 5:22

"...no man put a stumblingbock or an occasion to fall in his brother's way." Romans 14:13

"...we are ambassadors for Christ..." II Corinthians 5:20

Lies	Truths
I'm lonely, so I go to casinos to be around people.	Attend a friendly church and fellowship there.
I feel like I'm part of a group, like I belong and am accepted.	Be secure in Christ; if you accepted Christ, you're part of the best group of all—the family of God.
I'll invite my friends to go gambling with me, so they can have fun, too.	Do not play a part in getting anyone to start sinning or to continue sinning.
I enjoy a night out gambling with my friends; it's great entertainment.	Enjoy life in a godly way, as taking a walk with friends, visiting family, attending a concert of Christian music, having a hobby, participating in sports or watching sports at a school gym or game park.
Gambling at casinos is a good way to celebrate good happenings.	Celebrate God's blessing with a prayer or song of praise; invite friends to your home.
My friend got married today, so I'm going to the casino with a group of single women.	Pray for the newlyweds; get together at a restaurant.

I made a big sale today, so I'm going to enjoy a game of poker with the guys.	Thank God for the success; celebrate by enjoying an evening playing non-gambling games with the guys.
I have to go to the casino, because my friends and family want me to go there with them.	Don't please people by sinning; do please God by doing what He wants you to do.
I'll go to the casino to keep my friend company, even though I won't gamble.	Don't be a poor example for others or help them sin; be a godly role model to those addicted to gambling.

Section D

> Lie: Gambling is a good way to fill up my spare time.
> Truth: Use the time God gives you to lead others to Jesus and teach them God's wisdom.
> Colossians 4:5 "Walk in wisdom toward them that are without, redeeming the time."

"Redeeming the time, because the days are evil.
Wherefore be ye not unwise, but understanding what the will of the Lord is." Ephesians 5:16-17
"Go ye therefore, and teach all nations...
Teaching them to observe all things whatsoever I have commanded you..." Matthew 28:19-20
"...Go ye into all the world, and preach the gospel..."
Mark 16:15

"…repentance and remission of sins should be preached in his name among all nations…" Luke 24:47
"So then faith cometh by hearing, and hearing by the word of God." Romans 10:17
"…he that winneth souls is wise." Proverbs 11:30

Lies	Truths
Gambling is a great way to spend my spare time.	Gambling wastes precious minutes, hours, days, and weeks that God gives.
Gambling gets me out of the house.	You can get out of the house to serve God.
I'm retired and deserve the fun of gambling.	Satisfaction can be gained from serving God.
My wife won't miss me, So I'll stay a little longer.	Do not neglect your family.
My husband is unhappy with my gambling.	Do not disrupt your home life by gambling; it could result in divorce.
I know I'll miss church by going on this weekend gambling excursion, but I'll be sure to attend services next week.	Do not neglect to take time to worship God and meet your spiritual needs.
I'll just allow myself one hour at the slots.	Any amount of time spent gambling is a waste of time God has provided for you.
I'll stay a little longer.	Leave now—don't waste even one more minute of God's time.

Section E

> Lie: Gambling can have the good purposes of raising
> money for charities and schools and making more
> jobs.
> Truth: Raise charity funds and make more jobs in
> honest godly ways.
> Colossians 2:3-4 Know God's "...wisdom and knowledge.
> And this I say, lest any man should beguile you
> with enticing words."

"Let no man deceive you by any means..."
II Thessalonians 2:3
"Let no man deceive himself..." I Corinthians 3:18
"But let a man examine himself..." I Corinthians 11:28

Lies	Truths
Buy raffle tickets for a good cause.	Donate directly to the good cause instead.
We should have a raffle for a fundraiser.	Raise funds in a godly way instead.
It's a 50/50 drawing, and I can win half the money; if I don't win, my money will be a contribution.	Do you know who or what benefits from the other half of the money? If you want to contribute, do so outright without trying to win the paid drawing.

Play bingo, because the proceeds go to help abused people, senior citizens, scouts, a church.	Gambling for any purpose is a sin.
I should play the lotto, because, if I win, I can help the poor people, pay for a new church, etc.	You can give to the poor and to the church now with money that you have earned honestly.
The state can raise money for education by having a lotto.	The state can raise the funds another way, revise the budget, or operate within its current budget; having a lottery can lead to increased family problems and welfare costs.
Gambling helps charities and our state's finances.	Many of the profits of "charity gambling" are diverted from the "good cause"—often diverted to the income of the promoter or others who benefit in some way.
Gambling helps our state or country get out of debt.	Even if your country or state makes money with a lottery, most of its gambling citizens are losing their money.

| Gambling creates new jobs in the community and aids our economy. | The gambling industry does create some jobs, but many Are low-paying jobs and the higher-paying jobs are often given to re recruits from other places; much of the money from the tourists and even much of the money of local people is spent on the gambling, not on local businesses, so often the local businesses lose customers and have to layoff employees and sometimes are forced out of business; local restaurants and hotels often cannot compete with the low prices and convenience of the in-casino restaurants and hotel rooms which set low prices purposely to attract gamblers; local gamblers have less money to spend on food, clothing, bills, cars, recreation. |

Section F

Lie: It's my money, and I can use it to gamble.

Truth: It's God's money to use wisely in a way pleasing to God.

Haggai 2:8 "The silver is mine, and the gold is mine, saith the Lord of hosts."

"Wilt thou set thine eyes upon that which is not? For riches certainly make themselves wings; they fly away as an eagle toward heaven." Proverbs 23:5

Lies	Truths
I have plenty of money, so I can afford to lose.	God trusts us to use His money wisely.
I'll buy only five bingo cards; I won't miss a few quarters.	Don't buy any Bingo cards; don't waste any of God's money on games of chance.
I'll just use up the change in my pocket; because I don't like a pocket full of change.	If you don't like a pocket full of change, change the coins into paper money or higher value coins, and then you won't have a pocket full of coins—or give it to a needy person or charity.
I won a little on this lottery ticket, so I can buy two more tickets.	Never reinvest into gambling.
I get only one lottery ticket a week when I grocery shop.	Any amount of money— much or little—spent on lottery tickets is still gambling.
We play for only a quarter a game, so I lost only seventy-five cents.	Any misuse or waste of God's money is wrong.
The lottery card said, "Win up to $10,000 instantly."	The card should also say the other possibility: "Likely to lose your $2 instantly."

Take a chance—you might get lucky.	Don't risk losing God's money—gambling games are games of chance.
I win once in a while.	But how much do you lose?
I won big!	But how much have you lost over the years?
I didn't gamble away all that money—I must have counted my money wrong before I left the house.	Money vanishes faster than we realize when we gamble; as the verse says at the beginning of this section, "…For riches certainly make themselves wings; they fly away…" Proverbs 23:5 It is God's money that disappears!

Section G

> Lie: If I lose, I hurt only myself, not anyone else.
> Truth: You hurt God and others and yourself.
> Exodus 10:16 "…I have sinned against the Lord your God, and against you."

"…We have sinned against the Lord…….." I Samuel 7:6

Lies	Truths
I don't care if I lose; I only hurt myself.	Your gambling hurts many people, and it hurts God, too.

Gambling is legal where I live, so it is O. K. to gamble.	Gambling is legal in many places, but it is never acceptable by God; gambling is a sin, and sins hurt God.
Gambling isn't related to other law-breaking.	Theft, assault, sales of illegal drugs, prostitution, murder, and other crimes often flourish in gambling areas, due to the financial needs of the gamblers
Gambling does not hurt our country.	Much of gambling profit supports organized crime.
Nobody I know sees me.	God sees you, and any gambler is an ungodly role model for anyone watching them.
If I bring my "good luck" charm, I'll win.	Superstitions are sinful, and other people see the "good luck" charms.
So what if I lose—it's only money.	Have you lost time, bank account, house, car, job by your gambling? Have you lost your wife or husband or children by divorce caused by your gambling? Have you lost contact with other family members and friends by your gambling?

Section H

> Lie: It's O. K. for me to gamble, because I win more
>   often than I lose.
>
> Truth: Some people to win often, but these people win
>   at the expense of those who lose, and often those that
>   lose are rather poor; when you win at gambling, you
>   are getting your own money plus the money that
>   belonged to other people, and this is greed, and, in
>   a way, it is theft.
>
> Proverbs 17:11 "..he that getteth riches, and not by right,
>   shall leave them in the midst of his days, and at his
>   end shall be a fool."

"Rob not the poor…" Proverbs 22:22

"He that oppresseth the poor to increase his riches…shall surely come to want." Proverbs 22:16

"Whoso stoppeth his ears at the cry of the poor, he also shall cry himself, but shall not be heard." Proverbs 21:13

"He coveteth greedily all the day long: but the righteous giveth and spareth not." Proverbs 21:26

"Wealth gotten by vanity shall be diminished: but he that gathereth by labour shall increase." Proverbs 13:11

"He that is greedy of gain troubleth his own house…"
Proverbs 15:27

"My son, if sinners entice thee, consent thou not.

My son, walk not thou in the way with them; refrain thy foot from their path:

For their feet run to evil…

So are the ways of every one that is greedy of gain…"
Proverbs 1:10, 15-16,19
"…they are greedy dogs which can never have enough…they all look to their own way, every one for his gain…" Isaiah 56:11 (This verse doesn't refer specifically to gambling, but aptly describes gamblers.)

Lies	Truths
Don't think about the losers—just think about yourself.	This is a selfish greedy attitude.
It doesn't matter if others lose, so I can win.	It is wrong to provide for yourself or prosper at the expense of others.
So what if the other gamblers are poor—it's their choice to gamble.	Consider the poor and share with them—don't gamble and take what little they have.
It is alright to want to win at gambling.	It's never right to be greedy—to want your share, plus someone else's share; games of gambling are actually games of greed.

Section I

> Lie: I have enough money, but I want to be really rich and that is a good goal.
>
> Truth: We should have godly goals, not a goal of getting more and more and more money.
>
> Proverbs 28:20 "...he that maketh haste to be rich shall not be innocent."

"He that hasteth to be rich hath an evil eye, and considereth not that poverty shall come upon him." Proverbs 28:22

"...they that will be rich fall into temptation and a snare, and into many foolish and hurtful lusts, which drown men in destruction and perdition." I Timothy 6:9

"For the love of money is the root of all evil: which while some coveted after, they have erred from the faith, and pierced themselves through with many sorrows."
I Timothy 6:10

"He that loveth silver shall not be satisfied with silver; nor he that loveth abundance with increase: this is also vanity."
Ecclesiastes 5:10

"Lay not up for yourselves treasures upon earth..."
Matthew 6:19

"So is he that layeth up treasure for himself, and is not rich toward God." Luke 12:21

"But thou, O man of God, flee these things; and follow after righteousness, godliness, faith, love, patience, meekness." I Timothy 6:11

"I press toward the mark for the prize of the high calling of God in Christ Jesus." Philippians 3:14

"...seek ye first the kingdom of God, and his righteousness..." Matthew 6:33

"...lay up for yourselves treasures in heaven...
For where your treasure is, there will your heart be also." Matthew 6:20-21

"A good name is rather to be chosen than great riches, and loving favour rather than silver and gold." Proverbs 22:1 ("Favour" is kindness.)

"...Take heed, and beware of covetousness: for a man's life consisteth not in the abundance of the things which he possesseth." Luke 12:15

"...be content with such things as ye have..." Hebrews 13:5

"He that trusteth in his riches shall fall: but the righteous shall flourish..." Proverbs 11:28

Lies	Truths
I'm aiming to win the big jackpot.	Seek God instead and do works that follow you to heaven.
I'll be happy when I get richer.	Money never guarantees happiness and brings with it a set of problems unique to wealth, as the likely loss of privacy.
I'll be a millionaire someday—think how much I can win.	Face reality; the majority of gambling wins are small, few people make a million.

This money-making scheme will make me rich quick.	Few people get rich quick, and those who do are usually the schemers, themselves; most people lose more money than they make with get-rich-quick schemes.
I play the stock market to get rich fast.	Stock purchases should be done wisely with research and dependable professional advice, and as an investment, not as a way to get rich fast.
I'll place bigger bets and maybe I'll win more; I'll place more bets at a time and maybe win more.	Statistics show you are just likely to lose more.
I'll stop when I get $100, when I get $1,000, when I get a million dollars, when I get two million.	Gambling can be addictive; you say, "One win is not enough," when you begin to gamble compulsively; you won't stop until you say, "One play is too many."

Section J

Lie: If I keep trying, I will win, so somehow I'll get the money to gamble—even if I have to steal it.

Truth: It is never right to steal for any purpose—even if you did win with the stolen money and replaced it, stealing is still a sin.

Exodus 20:15 "Thou shalt not steal."

If you have already stolen, work with your hands to provide for the poor.

> Example: Help out at a charity thrift store that
>   gives clothes and furniture to the needy.
> Example: Work at a food pantry that gives to the
>   needy.
> Example: Repair a poor person's broken porch.
> Example: Build a ramp for a poor person that
>   walks with a cane.
> Example: Bake for a widow with children.
> Example: Mend and sew for a blind person who
>   has little money.
> Example: Knit baby sweaters for mothers who have
>   little money.

"Let him that stole steal no more: but rather let him labour, working with his hands the thing which is good, that he

Lies	Truths
My friend asked me to use his money to gamble, so it's O. K.	It's never O. K. to sin for somebody else—you will both be committing sin.

My son won't miss these coins from his piggy bank; my wife won't miss a few dollars from her purse; my husband won't miss a few dollars from his wallet; my boss won't miss a few dollars from the cash register.	Taking anything (or borrowing without permission) is theft.
My gambling money is all gone, so I'll get some cash with my credit card.	Save your credit card for real emergencies.
I can turn in my watch at the pawn shop and buy a better one when I win my money back.	Be satisfied with what you already have.
I'll take out a loan to win my money back.	Do not go into debt you might not repay; a loan is spending money you haven't yet earned.
I'll have to steal some money and jewelry to recoup my losses.	Stealing for any reason is a sin.
I'll sell some of my prescription pills to a drug addict to get money to keep gambling.	Do not deal in drugs; you'll just add another sin to the sin of gambling.
I'll take some money from the business account, so I can go back to the casino and make up my losses.	Embezzling is a form of theft, and stealing is a sin.

I can gamble with the grocery money; I will win it all back—and more; we'll have steaks this week	You're more likely to live on stale bread and water instead of steaks.
We don't need all that milk and fruit and vegetables this week; we'll have macaroni, and use the shopping money to gamble.	God expects us to take good care of our bodies by eating nutritional foods; don't neglect your body's needs to gamble.
I'll use the change from the grocery purchase and my gas purchase to buy lottery tickets.	Extra money can be a temptation to sin, but the money is still God's money and not meant for gambling purposes.
If you lend me some money to gamble, I'll pay you back after I win.	Do not make promises you might not be able to keep; there are no guarantees in gambling, and the odds are against you.

Section K

Lie: Gambling is not addictive, so I can quit gambling any time.

Truth: Gambling can easily become a way of life, a bad habit that is hard to break.

John 8:34 Jesus said, "…Whosoever committeth sin is the servant of sin."

"While they promise them liberty, they themselves are the servants of corruption: for of whom a man is overcome, of the same is he brought in bondage." II Peter 2:19

"But every man is tempted, when he is drawn away of his own lust, and enticed.

Then when lust hath conceived, it bringeth forth sin…" James 1:14-15

Lies	Truths
I won't get hooked on gambling.	Gambling addiction begins with the first bet in the poker game, the first nickel in the slots, the first bingo card, the first lottery ticket.
I'll never become a compulsive gambler.	Nobody can predict the future, so don't start.
The casino gives me $20 worth of quarters to start—it's part of the package deal along with the hotel room and meals; I'll only use the $20.	Once you start, it's hard to quit, especially if you are staying at the casino.
I have to play until I win. keep losing—except for	Statistics show you will an occasional small win tempt you to keep you playing.
I'll quit after I win back my $20.	You might never win back your money, and, if you do win, you'll be taking other people's money who lost.

I'll quit after my $50 is gone.	Gambling is addictive, so stop now.
Just this last quarter for bingo card.	Don't yield to temptation; stop now.
I've got a nickel left— I'll give the slots one more try.	Gambling is addictive, so stop now.
I won big tonight, so I'll go back tomorrow.	Gambling is addictive, so stop now.
I won, so I have to keep playing to win more.	You do not have to return to gambling for any reason.
I have to go back to the casino, because I lost a lot at blackjack.	Don't gamble to try to recoup losses or for any other reason.
This will be my last trip to the race track.	Stop the sin of gambling now.
I'll stop when my wife stops gambling.	People get convicted of sin at different times; the conviction has to come from within each person and based on the Bible.
I'll stop gambling to please my husband.	Stop gambling to please God, not to please a spouse or any other person; if you stop for the wrong reason, you are likely to regret the decision and resent the person you were trying to please.
Gambling isn't a problem for me.	Often we do not see ourselves objectively.

I know I'm a compulsive gambler, but I can handle a bingo game or a nickel slot machine or maybe I'll just watch.	Any gambling or even a gambling environment can get a compulsive gambler back into the habit.
I can stop gambling any time without help from anyone.	You will need the power of God and Bible truths to stop gambling, and you might need counseling to guide you or a support group to help you stick to your decision—to encourage you, to keep you accountable, to share ideas and obstacles and solutions.
I HAVE to buy a lottery ticket before the deadline.	You WANT to buy a lottery ticket, you don't have to buy a lottery ticket.
What if my lucky number is called and I haven't bought a ticket?	You will know you are a winner in the eyes of God by not committing the sin of gambling.

Section L

Lie: I can't stop gambling.
Truth: With God's help, I can stop.
Matthew 19:26 "…with God all things are possible."

"Is any thing too hard for the Lord?…" Genesis 18:14
"Ah Lord God…there is nothing too hard for thee…" Jeremiah 32:17

"For with God nothing shall be impossible." Luke 1:37
"I can do all things through Christ which strengtheneth me."
Philippians 4:13

"There hath no temptation taken you but such as is common to man: but God is faithful, who will not suffer you to be tempted above that ye are able; but will with the temptation also make a way to escape, that ye may be able to bear it." I Corinthians 10:13

"And ye shall know the truth, and the truth shall make you free." John 8:32
"Search the scriptures…" John 6:39
"Thy word have I hid in mine heart, that I might not sin against thee." Psalm 119:11

God says, "So shall my word be that goeth forth out of my mouth: it shall not return unto me void, but it shall accomplish that which I please, and it shall prosper in the thing whereto I sent it." Isaiah 5511 (This is God's promise that His words in the Bible will bring godly results.)

"…let a man examine himself…" I Corinthians 11:28
"…repentance to the acknowledging of the truth;
And that they may recover themselves out of the snare of the devil, who are taken captive by him at his will."
II Timothy 2:25-26
"If we confess our sins, he is faithful and just to forgive us our sins, and to cleanse us from all unrighteousness."

I John 1:9
"…sin no more." John 8:11

"My help cometh from the Lord…" Psalm 121:2
"In my distress I cried unto the Lord, and he heard me."
Psalm 120:1

"For God so loved the world, that he gave his only begotten
Son, that whosoever believeth in him should not perish, but
have everlasting life.
For God sent not his Son into the world to condemn the
world; but that the world through him might be saved.
He that believeth on him is not condemned…"
John 3:16-18

"…the gospel…
…how that Christ died for our sins according to the scriptures;
And that he was buried, and that he rose again the third day
according to the scriptures:
And that he was seen of Cephas, then of the twelve:
After that, he was seen of above five hundred brethren at
once…

And that, he was seen of James; then of all the apostles.
And last of all he was seen of me…" (Paul mentioned himself
last.) I Corinthians 15:1,3-8

"For by grace are ye saved through faith; and that not of
yourselves: it is the gift of God…" Ephesians 2:8

"But as many as received him to them gave he power to become the sons of God, even to them that believe on his name…" John 1:12

"For as many as are led by the Spirit of God, they are the sons of God." Romans 8:14

"And because ye are sons, God hath sent forth the Spirit of his So into your hearts, crying, Abba, Father."
Galatians 4:6

"For ye have not receive the spirit of bondage again to fear; but ye have received the Spirit of adoption, whereby we cry, Abba, Father." Romans 8:15

"…Our Father which art in heaven…" Matthew 6:9

If you are not a child of God, it is easy to become a child of God.

Do you believe John 3:16 quoted above?

Do you believe the verses from I Corinthians 15:1, 3-8 quoted above?

Do you want to accept God's Gift—His Son Jesus?

You can say this prayer now:

"Dear God, I agree with Your words in the Bible about salvation. I admit I am a sinner. I am sorry I sinned. I believe that You sent Jesus to die on the cross in payment for my sins. I believe He was buried and rose again and was seen by hundreds of people. Then He went back to live in heaven. I accept Your Gift of Jesus in payment for my sins and for everlasting life with You, God. Thank You for this Gift. Please help me be better for You. I pray in Jesus' Name, amen."

Welcome to the family of God.

Lies	Truths
I'm hooked on gambling forever.	With God's help, you CAN stop gambling.
God won't help me.	God will help you—reach out and ask Him for help; accept Christ as your Savior and become a child of God and keep praying—keep talking to Him, your heavenly Father.
I'm too deep into gambling to stop.	God can do anything; He can help you stop gambling.
I don't know how to begin to stop gambling.	Recognize you are a gambler, admit it to God, be sorry for for the sin of gambling, and ask God to forgive you.
I'll never be able to resist the temptation to gamble.	God will provide a way for you to resist temptation; Jesus will give you strength to resist temptation.
I'm not sure how to stay away from gambling.	God gives us Scriptures in the Bible to battle gambling; learn some Bible verses quoted throughout this topic about gambling and use them when you want to gamble; God promises that His Word will bring good godly results. GOD'S WORD WORKS!

Section M

> Lie: There's no future for me—I've lost everything gambling.
>
> Truth: God has a purpose for you—He wants you to do good works.
>
> Ephesians 2:10 "For we are his workmanship, created in Christ unto good works…"

"…brethren, ye have been called unto liberty; only use not liberty for an occasion to the flesh, but by love serve one another." Galatians 5:13

"…ready to every good work…" Titus 3:1

"That ye might walk worthy of the Lord unto all pleasing, being fruitful in every good work, and increasing in the knowledge of God…" Colossians 1:10

"…we ourselves also were sometimes foolish, disobedient, deceived, serving divers lusts and pleasures, living in malice and envy, hateful, and hating one another.

But after that the kindness and love of God our Savior toward man appeared,

Not by works of righteousness which we have done, but according to his mercy he saved us, by the washing of regeneration, and renewing of the Holy Ghost…"

Titus 3:3-5

"Know ye not that the unrighteous shall not inherit the kingdom of God?…

Nor thieves, nor covetous, nor drunkards, nor revilers, nor extortioners, shall inherit the kingdom of God.

And such were some of you: but ye are washed, but ye are sanctified, but ye are justified in the name of the Lord Jesus, and by the Spirit of our God." I Corinthians 6:9-11

"But now ye also put off all these; anger, wrath, malice, blasphemy, filthy communication out of your mouth.

…ye have put of the old man with his deeds;

And have put on the new man, which is renewed in knowledge after the image of him that created him…" Colossians 3:8-10

Paul said, "…I persecuted the church of God."
I Corinthians 15:9

Paul said, "…Christ Jesus came into the world to save sinners; of whom I am chief." I Timothy 1:15

God said, "…I have loved thee with an everlasting love…" Jeremiah 31:3

Paul said, "For I am persuaded, that neither death, nor life, nor angels, nor principalities, nor powers, nor things present, nor things to come,

Nor height, nor depth, nor any other creature, shall be able to separate us from the love of God, which is in Christ Jesus our Lord." Romans 8:38-39

The psalmist knew God is everywhere and said, "Whither shall I go from thy spirit? Or whither shall I flee from thy presence?

If I ascend up into heaven, thou are there: if I make my bed in hell, behold, thou art there.

If I take wings of the morning, and dwell in the uttermost parts of the sea;

Even there shall thy hand lead me, and thy right hand shall hold me." Psalm 139:7-10

The psalmist knew how much God cares and said, "O Lord, thou hast searched me, and known me.

Thou knowest my downsitting and mine uprising, thou understandest my my thought afaar off.

Thou compassest my path and my lying down, and art acquainted with all my ways.

For there is not a word in my tongue, but, lo, O Lord, thou knowest it altogether.

Thou hast beset me behind and before, and laid thine hand upon me." Psalm 139:1-5

"Trust in the Lord, and do good..." Psalm 37:3

"Commit thy way unto the Lord; trust also in him; and he shall bring it to pass." Psalm 37:5

"It is better to trust in the Lord than to put confidence in man." Psalm 118:8

"This book of the law shall not depart out of thy mouth; but thou shalt meditate therein day and night, that thou mayest observe to do according to all that is written therein: for then thou shalt make thy way prosperous, and then thou shalt have good success." Joshua 1:8

Lies	Truths
I'm worthless.	God has a purpose for you—to do good works for Him.
I'm too terrible to change.	You CAN change; other people were terrible sinners, but they changed and served God. Paul had even persecuted Christians, but he became a Christian, he preached the message of salvation to many people, and he taught other Christians how to lead people to Jesus and become the kind of people God wanted them to be.
I'm unwanted, unloved.	Even if people dislike you, God still loves you; you'll find some people love you, too.
I'm all alone.	God is everywhere.
I'm too afraid to start over.	Trust God to help you.
I'll never have any confidence.	Put your confidence in God, not in people—not in yourself or in other people.
I'll never be successful.	God promises you can learn to be a godly success by using the Bible.

INFORMATION ABOUT THE BIBLE

GOD'S WORD IS TRUE.
"…Lord…Thy word is true…" Psalm 119:159-160
"All scripture is given by the inspiration of God, and is profitable for doctrine, for reproof, for correction, for instruction in righteousness." II Timothy 3:16-17

KNOW GOD'S WORD.
"Search the scriptures…" John 5:39
"Thy word have I hid in mine heart, that I might not sin against thee." Psalm 119:11

USE GOD'S WORD.
"…be ye doers of the word…" James 1:22
"Be not wise in thine own eyes: fear the Lord and depart from evil."
It shall be health to thy navel, and marrow to thy bones." Proverbs 3:7-8

GOD GUARANTEES THAT HIS WORD WORKS.
God says, "So shall my word be that goeth forth out of my mouth: it shall not return unto me void, but it shall accomplish that which I please, and it shall prosper in the thing whereto I sent it." Isaiah 55:ll

This page may be reproduced without change and in its entirety to be used at Discover and Recover Club meetings and for noncommercial Christian purposes without prior permission from the author.
Games of a Gambler   Mary Goloversic Copyright   ©   2020 All rights reserved

USING GOD'S WORD BRINGS BLESSINGS.

"Happy is the man that findeth wisdom." Proverbs 3:1

"Blessed is the man that walketh not in the counsel of the ungodly, nor standeth in the way of sinners, nor sitteth in the seat of the scornful.

But his delight is in the law of the Lord; and in his law doth he meditate day and night.

And he shall be like a tree planted by the rivers of water, that bringeth forth his fruit in his season; his leaf also shall not wither; and whatsoever he doeth shall prosper."

Psalm 1:1-3

This page may be reproduced without change and in its entirety to be used at Discover and Recover Club meetings and for noncommercial Christian purposes without prior permission from the author.

Games of a Gambler   Mary Goloversic Copyright   ©   2020 All rights reserved

INFORMATION ABOUT GOD

GOD IS ALL-POWERFUL.

"Is any thing too hard for the Lord?..." Genesis 18:14

"...Lord God...there is nothing too hard for thee..." Jeremiah 32:17

"...with God nothing shall be impossible."
Luke 1:37

"...with God all things are possible." Mark 10:27

GOD WILL HELP YOU, INCLUDING PROVIDING A WAY FOR YOU TO OVERCOME TEMPTATION.

"There hath no temptation taken you
but such as is common to man:
but God is faithful,
who will not suffer you to be tempted
above that ye are able;
but will with the temptation
also make a way to escape,
that ye may be able to bear it."
I Corinthians 10:13

TRUST IN THE LORD.

"It is better to trust in the Lord than to put confidence in man." Psalm 118:8

This page may be reproduced without change and in its entirety to be used at Discover and Recover Club meetings and for noncommercial Christian purposes without prior permission from the author.

Games of a Gambler   Mary Goloversic Copyright   ©   2020 All rights reserved

"Trust in the Lord with all thine heart; and lean not unto thine own understanding.

In all thy ways acknowledge him, and he shall direct thy paths." Proverbs 3:5-6

"Trust in him at all times…" Psalm 62:8

This page may be reproduced without change and in its entirety to be used at Discover and Recover Club meetings and for noncommercial Christian purposes without prior permission from the author.

Games of a Gambler   Mary Goloversic Copyright   ©   2020 All rights reserved

INFORMATION ABOUT SALVATION, GOD'S GIFT—JESUS

In the Bible, God tells us all about the Gift He wants to give us; in the Bible, in the book of Romans, we can walk down the <u>Romans' Road</u> and listen to God tell us about His plan that provides a way for us to live in heaven.

<u>Romans 3:10, 23</u> "…There is none righteous…For all have sinned, and come short of the glory of God…"

> God knew that people did bad things long ago and still do bad things today; we think bad thoughts, say bad words, and do bad actions— these are our sins. (Also see Romans 5:12.)

<u>Romans 6:23</u> "For the wages of sin is death; but the gift of God is eternal life through Jesus Christ our Lord."

> The punishment for sin is to go to hell; we deserve punishment in hell.
>
> God does not want us to go to hell when we die; He wants us to live forever in heaven with Him, but we need to be pure for heaven.

<u>Romans 5:8</u> "But God commendeth his love toward us, in that, while we were yet sinners, Christ died for us."

> God showed His love for us by sending His Son to shed His blood and to die on the cross to pay the punishment for all the bad things

This page may be reproduced without change and in its entirety to be used at Discover and Recover Club meetings and for noncommercial Christian purposes without prior permission from the author.

<u>Games of a Gambler</u>   Mary Goloversic Copyright   ©   2020 All rights reserved

we do—to save us from punishment in hell.
<u>Romans 10:9-10,13</u> "That thou shalt confess with thy
mouth the Lord Jesus, and shalt believe in thine
heart that God hath raised him from the dead, thou
shalt be saved. For with the heart man believeth unto
righteousness; and with the mouth confession is made
unto salvation…For whosoever shall call upon the
name of the Lord shall be saved."

God sent His Son, Jesus, to pay for our sins.
"For God so loved the world, that he gave his only
begotten Son, that whosoever believeth in him should
not perish, but have everlasting life." (John 3:16)

God's plan to pay for our sins is good news for us and is told
in the gospel (good message, good news).
"…the gospel…how Christ died for our sins according
to the scriptures;
And that he was buried, and that he rose again the third
day…
And that he was seen…of above five hundred brethren
at once…" (I Corinthians 15:1, 3-6)

We all sin—do things that hurt God and hurt people and
even hurt our own selves.

This page may be reproduced without change and in its entirety to be used at Discover and
Recover Club meetings and for noncommercial Christian purposes without prior permission
from the author.
<u>Games of a Gambler</u>   Mary Goloversic Copyright   ©   2020 All rights reserved

"Salvation" is Jesus saving us from punishment in hell to pay for our sins.

> He came "…to save…" (Luke 19:10)

Jesus paid for our sins on the cross.

> "Who his own self bare our sins in his own body on
> the tree…" (I Peter 2:24)

This free payment is a gift we can receive.

> "… it is the gift of God…." (Ephesians 2:8)

If we accept this Gift—Jesus Christ, we are saved from hell.

> "He that believeth on him is not condemned…"
> (John 3:18)

If we accept this Gift, we should not brag about it, but give God the glory.

> "For by grace are ye saved through faith; and that
> not of yourselves: it is the gift of God:
> Not of works, lest any man should boast."
> (Ephesians 2:8-9)
> We did not work for the Gift; we did not pay for the
> Gift; Jesus did; we should thank and praise Him.

We should tell other people how to get this Gift; Jesus wants everyone to come to Him, including children.

> "…Go ye into all the world, and preach the gospel…"
> (Mark 16:15)

This page may be reproduced without change and in its entirety to be used at Discover and Recover Club meetings and for noncommercial Christian purposes without prior permission from the author.

Games of a Gambler   Mary Goloversic Copyright   ©   2020 All rights reserved

He told adults to let "…little children to come unto me…." (Luke 18:16)

Nobody should wait to accept God's Gift—Jesus.
"…now is the accepted time; behold, now is the day of salvation…" (II Corinthians 6:2)
Note that the verse says **now**, not tomorrow, not sometime in the future.

We all like gifts; God offers us His Son, Jesus, the Best Gift. Jesus is God's Gift to us—for you and for me, and we need to do is tell God that we accept His Gift, Jesus, as our Savior for our sins.

We have to **<u>repent</u>** our sins, **<u>believe</u>** the gospel message, and **<u>receive</u>** Jesus.
"…repent ye, and believe the gospel."
(Mark 16:15)

Are you sorry for your sins?
Do you believe in Jesus
as YOUR Savior?
Do you want to accept Jesus
as YOUR Savior to pay for YOUR sins?
Accept Jesus **<u>now</u>** by saying this prayer.

This page may be reproduced without change and in its entirety to be used at Discover and Recover Club meetings and for noncommercial Christian purposes without prior permission from the author.
<u>Games of a Gambler</u>   Mary Goloversic Copyright   ©   2020 All rights reserved

"Dear God, I agree with Your Words in the Bible about salvation. I admit I am a sinner. I am sorry I sinned. I believe that You sent Jesus to die on the cross in payment for my sins. I believe Jesus rose from the dead on the third day. Then Jesus stayed on earth many days, and He was seen by hundreds of people. Then He went up to live in heaven. I accept Your Gift of Jesus in payment for my sins and for everlasting life with You, God. Thank You for Jesus, the Best Gift. Please help me travel to success—to be the person You want me to be in Jesus' Name, amen."

Your name _____

Today's date_____

You can look up other Bible verses about accepting Jesus as your Savior: John 3:7, Luke 18:16, Acts 1:2-3, Acts 16:30-31, I Peter 2:24, I John 4:9

This page may be reproduced without change and in its entirety to be used at Discover and Recover Club meetings and for noncommercial Christian purposes without prior permission from the author.

Games of a Gambler   Mary Goloversic Copyright   ©   2020 All rights reserved

INFORMATION ABOUT SUCCESS

success=being the person God want you to be,
    not what you or others want you to be

*   *   *

Accepting Jesus Christ is the beginning of success.

*   *   *

Each step involves God, others and you.

*   *   *

You cannot change others, but you can change yourself,
and others can learn from the changes in you.

*   *   *

"This book of the law shall not depart out of thy mouth;
    but thou shalt meditate therein day and night,
that thou mayest observe to do
    according to all that is written therein:
for then thou shalt make thy way prosperous, and
    then thou shalt have good success."
Joshua 1:8

This page may be reproduced without change and in its entirety to be used at Discover and Recover Club meetings and for noncommercial Christian purposes without prior permission from the author.

Games of a Gambler   Mary Goloversic Copyright   ©   2020 All rights reserved

Lies lead to failure.
Truths lead to success.

You will hear lies all your life—
    probably every day,
    in any place,
    in all sorts of ways—
so you need to keep doing the 8 steps to success whenever
lies appear—
    from Satan or
    from other people or
    from yourself or
    from the world.

Start toward success by asking yourself,
    "What is Satan's lie in MY life today?"

8 STEPS TO SUCCESS (step titles)

1. **READ BIBLE TRUTHS**
2. **RECOGNIZE**
3. **REPENT**
4. **REPLACE**
5. **LOVE**
6. **FORGIVE**
7. **COMMUNICATE**
8. **HELP**

This page may be reproduced without change and in its entirety to be used at Discover and Recover Club meetings and for noncommercial Christian purposes without prior permission from the author.

Games of a Gambler   Mary Goloversic Copyright   ©   2020 All rights reserved

8-STEPS TO SUCCESS (WITH DETAILS AND SCRIPTURES)

1. READ BIBLE TRUTHS leading to godly success in my life; believe the Bible.
"Search the scriptures…" (John 5:39)
"…Lord…thy word is true…"
(Psalm 119:159-160)
"..it was impossible for God to lie..."
(Hebrews 6:18)

2. RECOGNIZE LIES leading to sinful failure in my life.
"…Satan…deceiveth the whole world..."
(Revelation 12:9)
"Let no man deceive you…"
(II Thessalonians 2:3)
"Let no man deceive himself…"
(I Corinthians 3:18)
"…let a man examine himself..."
(I Corinthians 11:28)

3. REPENT of the sins based on the lies I believed.
"…I will be sorry for my sin." (Psalm 38:18)
"...repentance to the acknowledging of the

This page may be reproduced without change and in its entirety to be used at Discover and Recover Club meetings and for noncommercial Christian purposes without prior permission from the author.

Games of a Gambler   Mary Goloversic Copyright   ©   2020 All rights reserved

truth...that they may recover themselves
out of the snare of the devil..."
(II Timothy 2:25-26)

4. REPLACE my sinful thoughts, words, and
actions with godly thoughts, words, and
actions.
"...put off...the old man...put on the new man...
"Neither give place to the devil."
(Ephesians 4:22,24,27)

5. LOVE—"...love one another..." (John 15:12)
Love God
Love others
Love myself in a healthy, not self-centered, way
Accept God's love
Accept brotherly love from others

6. FORGIVE—"...forgiving one another..."
(Ephesians 4:32)
Forgive others, even is they don't ask (Give the
gift of forgiveness.)
Forgive myself
Ask God to forgive me (salvation and confession)
Ask people to forgive me
Accept the gift of forgiveness from God

This page may be reproduced without change and in its entirety to be used at Discover and
Recover Club meetings and for noncommercial Christian purposes without prior permission
from the author.
Games of a Gambler   Mary Goloversic Copyright   ©   2020 All rights reserved

Accept the gift of forgiveness from people

7. COMMUNICATE—"...speaking the truth in love,,," (Ephesians 4:15)
Communicate with God (talk in prayer and listen in the Bible)
Communicate with people in an honest loving way (talk, listen, and respond).
Communicate with myself in an honest loving way

8. HELP—"...come and help..." (Luke 5:7)
Help God
Help others
Help myself
Ask for and accept God's help
Ask for and accept help from others

This page may be reproduced without change and in its entirety to be used at Discover and Recover Club meetings and for noncommercial Christian purposes without prior permission from the author.

Games of a Gambler   Mary Goloversic Copyright   ©   2020 All rights reserved

USING THE 8 STEPS TO SUCCESS TO STOP GAMBLING.

Look over the information boxes A-M (located a few pages past this page) and decide which box has the gambling lie that most influenced you to gamble.

Use this box as you go through steps 1-8.

Step 1: **R**ead the Bible

In the information box you chose, look at the Bible quotation in the box that combats the gambling lie that most influences you.

> "Search the scriptures…" John 5:39
>
> "And ye shall know the truth, and the truth will make you free." John 8:32

Step 2: **R**ecognize lie

Look over the lie in that box and be honest with yourself as you do this self-check.

> "…let a man examine himself…" I Corinthians 11:28
>
> "Let no man deceive himself…" I Corinthians 3:18
>
> "Let no man deceive you…" II Thessalonians 2:3

Step 3: **R**epent

Repent of the sin of gambling based on the gambling lie you believed to get out of the gambling trap—admit the sin of

This page may be reproduced without change and in its entirety to be used at Discover and Recover Club meetings and for noncommercial Christian purposes without prior permission from the author.

Games of a Gambler   Mary Goloversic Copyright   ©   2020 All rights reserved

gambling and be sorry for it and confess it to God to be free from the guilt of the sin of gambling.

> "…repentance to the acknowledging of the truth; …that they may recover themselves out of the snare of the devil…" II Timothy 2:25-26
>
> "If we confess our sins, he is faithful and just to forgive us our sins, and to cleanse us from all unrighteousness." I John 1:9

Step 4: Replace

Replacement is also part of the plan to stop gambling.

Each gambler needs to turn from gambling and turn to God; they need to replace the sin of gambling with God's good ways.

I Timothy 6:11 gives some suggestions; we are to flee the love of money and other such sins "…and follow after righteousness, godliness, faith, love, patience, meekness."

Step 5: Love

Accept God's love and brotherly love from others, love God and people, love yourself in a healthy, not self-centered way.

Step 6: Forgive

Forgive others and forgive yourself, ask for forgiveness from God and from people, accept the gift of forgiveness from God and from people, including yourself.

This page may be reproduced without change and in its entirety to be used at Discover and Recover Club meetings and for noncommercial Christian purposes without prior permission from the author.

Games of a Gambler   Mary Goloversic Copyright   ©   2020 All rights reserved

Step 7: Communicate
Communicate with God—talking in prayer and listening in the Bible, communicate with others in an honest loving way—talk, listen, and respond), communicate with yourself in an honest loving way.

Step 8: Help
Ask for and accept help from God and from people, help God, others, and yourself.

REPEAT THIS PROCESS BY CHOOSING A BOX WITH ANOTHER LIE THAT INFLUENCES YOU TO GAMBLE AND REPEAT THE PROCESS OF USING THE 8 STEPS.

KEEP DOING THIS FOR AS MANY OF THE BOXES WITH LIES THAT INFLUENCE YOU TO GAMBLE.

This page may be reproduced without change and in its entirety to be used at Discover and Recover Club meetings and for noncommercial Christian purposes without prior permission from the author.
Games of a Gambler   Mary Goloversic Copyright   ©   2020 All rights reserved

FOUR QUESTIONS TO USE WITH INFORMATION BOXES A-M

The following information can be used for a personal study, at a book club, as a basis for "Using the 8 Steps to Success to Stop Gambling," or as a basis for a group meetings—Gambling Workshop and "D & R Club" ("Discover and Recover Club" —**d**iscover and **r**ecover—discover the truths and recover from the lies).

This type of study can help you gain godly insights and apply the biblical wisdom in your life and help others do the same. Even if you do not gamble, you can do this.

Use the information in each of the boxes A-M to answer the four questions. To do this more easily for personal study or at a book club, make a handwritten copy of the questions or copy them on a copying machine.

Question 1 about my past failure:
   What did I ever think or say or do that the lie says?

Question 2 about my past success:
   What did I ever think or say or do that the truth says?

Question 3 about my present success:
   How did I make progress to success

This page may be reproduced without change and in its entirety to be used at Discover and Recover Club meetings and for noncommercial Christian purposes without prior permission from the author.

Games of a Gambler   Mary Goloversic Copyright   ©   2020 All rights reserved

recently by applying God's truth in the
last information box I read?

Question 4 about my plans for more success:

What do I plan to think or say or do now to
carry out the truth in today's information box?

This page may be reproduced without change and in its entirety to be used at Discover and Recover Club meetings and for noncommercial Christian purposes without prior permission from the author.

Games of a Gambler   Mary Goloversic Copyright   ©   2020 All rights reserved

GAMBLING INFORMATION—BOXES A-M

SECTIONS A-M INFORMATION BOXES OF LIES AND TRUTHS AND SCRIPTURES ABOUT GAMBLING TO BE USED AT "DISCOVER AND RECOVER CLUB" ("D & R CLUB") MEETINGS, BOOK CLUB MEETINGS, AND FOR PERSONAL USE (taken from <u>Games of a Gambler</u> and the Bible)

(These pages can be copied
for non-commercial Christian purposes.)

Section A

Lie: Gambling is just a way to have fun—games for people of all ages.

Truth: Games of gambling are games of chance—taking a risk of losing your money to win the money of others, and losing money is not pleasurable, not fun; you seldom see smiles at casinos, gambling card games, etc.—even quarrels can erupt.

Proverbs 21:17 "He that loveth pleasure shall be a poor man..."

This page may be reproduced without change and in its entirety to be used at Discover and Recover Club meetings and for noncommercial Christian purposes without prior permission from the author.

<u>Games of a Gambler</u>   Mary Goloversic Copyright   ©   2020 All rights reserved

Section B

Lie: Gambling will solve my money problems and even
  some of my other problems.
Truth: Gambling won't solve your problems, and
  will cause other problems, so use the Bible
  to solve your problems—work hard, budget your
  money to cover your basis needs, and skip your
  "wants."
Proverbs 3:5-6 "Trust in the Lord with all thine heart;
  and lean not unto thine own understanding.
  In all thy ways acknowledge him, and he shall direct
  thy paths."

Section C

Lie: Gambling is a good way to socialize; my friends and
family expect me to gamble with them.
Truth: God provides godly ways to socialize,
such at attending church and visiting friends; don't
gamble to please people—stop gambling to please
God; gambling with friends and family sets a bad
example for them and for others..
Hebrews 10:25 "Not forsaking the assembling of ourselves
together…"

This page may be reproduced without change and in its entirety to be used at Discover and Recover Club meetings and for noncommercial Christian purposes without prior permission from the author.

Games of a Gambler   Mary Goloversic Copyright   ©   2020 All rights reserved

Section D

Lie: Gambling is a good way to fill up my spare time.

Truth: Use the time God gives you to lead others to
Jesus and teach them God's wisdom.

Colossians 4:5 "Walk in wisdom toward them that are
without, redeeming the time."

Section E

Lie: Gambling can have the good purposes of raising
money for charities and schools and making more
jobs.

Truth: Raise charity funds and make more jobs in
honest godly ways.

Colossians 2:3-4 Know God's "…wisdom and knowledge.
And this I say, lest any man should beguile you
with enticing words."

This page may be reproduced without change and in its entirety to be used at Discover and Recover Club meetings and for noncommercial Christian purposes without prior permission from the author.

Games of a Gambler   Mary Goloversic Copyright   ©   2020 All rights reserved

Section F

Lie: It's my money, and I can use it to gamble.
Truth: It's God's money to use wisely in a way pleasing
to God.
Haggai 2:8 "The silver is mine, and the gold is mine,
saith the Lord of hosts."

Section G

Lie: If I lose, I hurt only myself, not anyone else.
Truth: You hurt God and others and yourself.
Exodus 10:16 "…I have sinned against the Lord your God,
and against you."

This page may be reproduced without change and in its entirety to be used at Discover and Recover Club meetings and for noncommercial Christian purposes without prior permission from the author.

Games of a Gambler   Mary Goloversic Copyright   ©   2020 All rights reserved

Section H

Lie: It's O. K. for me to gamble, because I win more
    often than I lose.
Truth: Some people to win often, but these people win
    at the expense of those who lose, and often those that
    lose are rather poor; when you win at gambling, you
    are getting your own money plus the money that
    belonged to other people, and this is greed, and, in
    a way, it is theft.
Proverbs 17:11 "..he that getteth riches, and not by right,
    shall leave them in the midst of his days, and at his
    end shall be a fool."

Section I

Lie: I have enough money, but I want to be really rich and
    that is a good goal.
Truth: We should have godly goals, not a goal of getting
    more and more and more money.
Proverbs 28:20 "...he that maketh haste to be rich shall not
    be innocent."

This page may be reproduced without change and in its entirety to be used at Discover and Recover Club meetings and for noncommercial Christian purposes without prior permission from the author.
Games of a Gambler   Mary Goloversic Copyright   ©   2020 All rights reserved

Section J

Lie: If I keep trying, I will win, so somehow I'll get the money to gamble—even if I have to steal it.
Truth: It is never right to steal for any purpose—even if you did win with the stolen money and replaced it, stealing is still a sin.
Exodus 20:15 "Thou shalt not steal."

Section K

Lie: Gambling is not addictive, so I can quit gambling any time.
Truth: Gambling can easily become a way of life, a bad habit that is hard to break.
John 8:34 Jesus said, "…Whosoever committeth sin is the servant of sin."

Section L

Lie: I can't stop gambling.
Truth: With God's help, I can stop.
Matthew 19:26 "…with God all things are possible."

This page may be reproduced without change and in its entirety to be used at Discover and Recover Club meetings and for noncommercial Christian purposes without prior permission from the author.
Games of a Gambler   Mary Goloversic Copyright   ©   2020 All rights reserved

Section M

Lie: There's no future for me—I've lost everything
gambling.

Truth: God has a purpose for you—He wants you to do
good works.

Ephesians 2:10 "For we are his workmanship, created in
Christ unto good works..."

This page may be reproduced without change and in its entirety to be used at Discover and Recover Club meetings and for noncommercial Christian purposes without prior permission from the author.

Games of a Gambler   Mary Goloversic Copyright   ©   2020 All rights reserved

DISCOVER AND RECOVER (D & R) CLUB
FOR GAMBLING—MATERIALS

Make copies of the "Success and Salvation" pamphlet (located at the end of the book) to give to new members.

If possible, have a Bible and a copy of <u>Games of a Gambler</u> for each member. Also extra pamphlets to give to others.

If there are not enough books for everyone, make copies of these D & R Club Meeting pages and the song and staple them together. The author grants you permission to copy these pages for noncommercial Christian use.

If there are not enough books, make copies of the previous section, Gambling Information-Boxes A-M, for each person who does not have a book. Staple these pages together. The author grants you permission to copy these pages for noncommercial Christian use.

Provide 4" X 6" note cards (or 4' X 6" pieces of paper and pencil or pens for each person.

Pass out the materials before the meeting begins.

Members can take turns being group leader—all the leader has to do is read the information in **bold** print.

Before the meeting begins, the leader should check on the page number of the information covered at the last meeting to use for the Progress Question.

This page may be reproduced without change and in its entirety to be used at Discover and Recover Club meetings and for noncommercial Christian purposes without prior permission from the author.

<u>Games of a Gambler</u>   Mary Goloversic Copyright   ©   2020 All rights reserved

DISCOVER AND RECOVER (D & R) CLUB FOR GAMBLING—MEETING

The leader reads the sentences in bold print.
The capitalized words in regular print are section dividers and to not have to be read.
Leader and club members read the sentences in regular print.
The other regular print sentences phrases in *italics* are directions.

WELCOME

Welcome to the meeting of the Discover and Recover Club.

In this club, we <u>discover</u> God's truths and use these truths to recognize lies and <u>recover</u> from the gambling habit.

> *(If there are new members, give them a copy of the success pamphlet and bookmark.)*

Are there any announcements?

OPENING PRAYER

We will begin with a prayer.

"Dear God,

Thank You for bringing us together. We know You are the Most Holy. We love You, God. We are glad You love us, even when we behave badly.

We know we sin—we think bad things, say bad

This page may be reproduced without change and in its entirety to be used at Discover and Recover Club meetings and for noncommercial Christian purposes without prior permission from the author.

<u>Games of a Gambler</u>   Mary Goloversic Copyright   ©   2020 All rights reserved

things, and do bad things. We are sorry for the sins we <u>silently</u> tell you about now…..

For things You have done for others and for us, God, we <u>take turns</u> telling You <u>out loud</u> our praises and thanks now…..

We <u>take turns</u> telling You <u>out loud</u> our requests for the needs of others and ourselves now….. Thank You for helping us break out gambling.

Please help us to have a good meeting to discover your truths and use them to recover from our gambling.

We pray in Jesus' Name, amen."

PROGRESS QUESTION

Open your copies of the book, <u>Games of a Gambler</u>, and turn to the back of the book and find the boxed information for the diary entry we read at the last meeting.

> *(Give the page number of the topic and allow time for the people to find the topic information.)*

How did you make progress to success by applying God's truth in the last meeting's information box?

> (Be sure the members share the talking time; don't spend more than a total of 10 minutes on this part of the meeting.)

This page may be reproduced without change and in its entirety to be used at Discover and Recover Club meetings and for noncommercial Christian purposes without prior permission from the author.

Games of a Gambler   Mary Goloversic Copyright   ©   2020 All rights reserved

REVIEW OF THE 8 STEPS TO SUCCESS

We will now read the 8 steps to success together.

1. Read Bible
2. Recognize lies
3. Repent
4. Replace
5. Love
6. Forgive
7. Communicate
8. Help

Read with whom we do the 8 steps.

with God, others, and ourselves

Whom can we change?

We can only change ourselves, not others, but others can learn from the godly changes in us.

REVIEW OF LIES AND TRUTHS

For what hurtful things should we look in our lives?

lies

Who tells lies?

Satan

other people

us

This page may be reproduced without change and in its entirety to be used at Discover and Recover Club meetings and for noncommercial Christian purposes without prior permission from the author.

Games of a Gambler   Mary Goloversic Copyright   ©   2020 All rights reserved

Let's read together what the Bible has to say about lies.

"…the devil…is a liar, and the father of it."
John 8:44

"…Satan which deceiveth the whole world…"
Revelation 12:9

"…Jesus…said…Take heed that no man deceive
you." Matthew 24:4

"Let no man deceive himself…" I Corinthians 3:18

"Trust ye not in lying words…" Jeremiah 7:4

Who always tells the truth?

God

What does the Bible say about God and truth?

"…God, that cannot lie…" Titus 1:2

"…put your trust in the Lord." Psalm 4:5

We all have to recognize the lies we hear and the lies we tell that lead first to one failure and then further failure.

We need to stop believing lies and start believing God's truths.

READING OF THE DISCOVER & RECOVER BOXED
INFORMATION

Turn to today's information box in Section _____.

Everybody please read this information together.

This page may be reproduced without change and in its entirety to be used at Discover and Recover Club meetings and for noncommercial Christian purposes without prior permission from the author.

Games of a Gambler   Mary Goloversic Copyright   ©   2020 All rights reserved

COPYING THE BOXED INFORMATION AND READING TODAY'S SCRIPTURE IN THE BIBLE

Please take you note card and pen (or note paper, pencil) **and copy the information for today's diary entry page (or, for those who do not have a book, use the staples copies of information boxes).**

When you finish, please use a Bible and look up the Scripture you have copied on today's note card; if you finish early, continue reading in the chapter you found the Scripture. Also, you can begin to memorize the Scripture.

DISCUSSION TIME

You can close the book and Bible now; if you have borrowed them, will you please pass them over to me?

(Allow time to pass in the books and Bibles.)

Now look at your note card.

We will now answer three questions related to today's diary entry information copied on your note card.

(All some time for each question, but no more than a total of 10 minutes per question.)

<u>Question 1</u> is about our past failures:

What did I ever think or say or do that the lie says?

<u>Question 2</u> relates to our past success:

What did I ever think or say or do that the truth says?

This page may be reproduced without change and in its entirety to be used at Discover and Recover Club meetings and for noncommercial Christian purposes without prior permission from the author.

Games of a Gambler   Mary Goloversic Copyright   ©   2020 All rights reserved

<u>Question 3</u> covers our plans for more success:
    What did I plan to think or say or do now to
    carry out the truth?

Bring this note card home with you and use God's truth in your life.

SAYING THE CHEER
We will say the words of "Give Up Gambling."

Give up, give up, give up gambling.
Give up, give up, give up gambling.
Give up, give up, give up gambling.
Yes! Yes! Yes! Now! Now! Now!

PRAYERS

We will close the meeting with prayer.

<u>Note to Leader: Use the following salvation information at the first meeting and at any other meetings that have new members. Otherwise, go on to the Prayer of Confession and Closing Prayer.</u>

<u>Information about salvation</u>

First, though, I want to talk to you about Jesus.
You need Jesus to help you to stop gambling.

This page may be reproduced without change and in its entirety to be used at Discover and Recover Club meetings and for noncommercial Christian purposes without prior permission from the author.

<u>Games of a Gambler</u>   Mary Goloversic Copyright   ©   2020 All rights reserved

You need Jesus to get into heaven.

Long ago God, the Father, sent Jesus, His Son, from heaven to earth to shed His blood dying on the cross to cover your sins, to pay for your sins.

Listen to God's promise in John 3:16 of the Bible.
"For God so loved the world, that he have his
only begotten Son that whosoever believeth in
Him should not perish, but have everlasting life."

In I Corinthians 15:1-6 of the Bible, God explains more about what Jesus did.
"...the gospel...
By which also ye are saved...
...how that Christ died for our sins...
And that he was buried, and that he rose again
the third day...
And that he was seen...of above five hundred
brethren at once..."

John 3:16 says God gave His Son.
God offers YOU payment for your sins by accepting God's Gift—Jesus.
This Gift must be accepted to become YOUR Gift.
Do YOU believe Jesus died for your sins, was buried, and rose again to live with God, the Father, in heaven?

This page may be reproduced without change and in its entirety to be used at Discover and Recover Club meetings and for noncommercial Christian purposes without prior permission from the author.
Games of a Gambler   Mary Goloversic Copyright   ©   2020 All rights reserved

**If you do, you can accept Jesus now by praying
the prayer I read to you now.
Please bow your heads and close your eyes.
I will pause every few words, so you can silently
repeat the words to God.**

"Dear God, (pause)

I know that I sin. (pause)
I think **bad thoughts,** (pause) **say bad things,** (pause)
do bad things. (pause)
I hurt You, others, and myself. (pause)
I am sorry for all my sins. (pause)

**I believe Your words in the Bible.
I believe that You sent Jesus** (pause) **to die on the cross**
(pause) **to pay for my sins.** *(pause)*
I believe He was buried, *(pause)* **rose again,** *(pause)*
returned to earth for a while, *(italics)* **and now lives in
heaven.** *(pause)*

I accept Your Gift of Jesus *(pause)* **in payment for my sins**
(pause) **and for everlasting life with you.** *(pause)*

Thank You for this Gift of Jesus *(pause)* **for my Savior. In
Jesus' Name, amen."** *(pause)*

This page may be reproduced without change and in its entirety to be used at Discover and
Recover Club meetings and for noncommercial Christian purposes without prior permission
from the author.
Games of a Gambler   Mary Goloversic Copyright   ©   2020 All rights reserved

Prayer of confession

Please bow your heads and look at the prayer.
If you want to confess YOUR sin of gambling to God,
silently read this prayer while I read the prayer aloud.
(read the confession prayer aloud)
Dear God,
I realize I was wrong to gamble. I misused Your money by
losing it gambling and helped others misuse Your money
by winning money from them. I am sorry for gambling.

Keeping your heads bowed, please close your eyes while
I read the closing prayer.
(read the closing prayer)

Closing prayer

"Dear God,
Thank You for Your truths in the Bible to guide us to
break the habit of gambling. Thank you for any progress
we have made.
Help us to keep private the confidential comments people
shared today. Help as we apply Your Truths found in
today's Scripture.
Please give us strength to say 'no' to gambling.
Help us keep looking up to You.
In Jesus' Name, amen."

This page may be reproduced without change and in its entirety to be used at Discover and Recover Club meetings and for noncommercial Christian purposes without prior permission from the author.

Games of a Gambler   Mary Goloversic Copyright   ©   2020 All rights reserved

GAMBLING WORKSHOP—MATERIALS

Materials needed for a Gambling Workshop

At least one copy of the book, Games of a Gambler and a copy of the Bible, and, for each person, paper, pens/pencils, copies of the following information and the "Success and Salvation" pamphlet at the end of the book.

(If some people do not have a copy of the book, Games of a Gambler, copy these pages of information boxes and staple them together for each person in the workshop who does not have a copy of Games of a Gambler.)

Section A

> Lie: Gambling is just a way to have fun—games for people of all ages.
>
> Truth: Games of gambling are games of chance—taking a risk of losing your money to win the money of others, and losing money is not pleasurable, not fun; you seldom see smiles at casinos, gambling card games, etc.—even quarrels can erupt.
>
> Proverbs 21:17 "He that loveth pleasure shall be a poor man…"

This page may be reproduced without change and in its entirety to be used at Discover and Recover Club meetings and for noncommercial Christian purposes without prior permission from the author.

Games of a Gambler   Mary Goloversic Copyright   ©   2020 All rights reserved

Section B

Lie: Gambling will solve my money problems and even some of my other problems.

Truth: Gambling won't solve you problems, and will cause other problems, so use the Bible to solve your problems—work hard, budget your money to cover your basis needs, and skip your "wants."

Proverbs 3:5-6 "Trust in the Lord with all thine heart; and lean not unto thine own understanding. In all thy ways acknowledge him, and he shall direct thy paths."

Section C

Lie: Gambling is a good way to socialize; my friends and family expect me to gamble with them.

Truth: God provides godly ways to socialize, such at attending church and visiting friends; don't gamble to please people—stop gambling to please God; gambling with friends and family sets a bad example for them and for others..

Hebrews 10:25 "Not forsaking the assembling of ourselves together…"

This page may be reproduced without change and in its entirety to be used at Discover and Recover Club meetings and for noncommercial Christian purposes without prior permission from the author.

Games of a Gambler   Mary Goloversic Copyright   ©   2020 All rights reserved

Section F

Lie: It's my money, and I can use it to gamble.
Truth: It's God's money to use wisely in a way pleasing
to God.
Haggai 2:8 "The silver is mine, and the gold is mine,
saith the Lord of hosts."

Section H

Lie: It's O. K. for me to gamble, because I win more
often than I lose.
Truth: Some people to win often, but these people win
at the expense of those who lose, and often those that
lose are rather poor; when you win at gambling, you
are getting your own money plus the money that
belonged to other people, and this is greed, and, in
a way, it is theft.
Proverbs 17:11 "..he that getteth riches, and not by right,
shall leave them in the midst of his days, and at his
end shall be a fool."

This page may be reproduced without change and in its entirety to be used at Discover and
Recover Club meetings and for noncommercial Christian purposes without prior permission
from the author.
Games of a Gambler   Mary Goloversic Copyright   ©   2020 All rights reserved

Section I

Lie: I have enough money, but I want to be really rich and that is a good goal.
Truth: We should have godly goals, not a goal of getting more and more and more money.
Proverbs 28:20 "…he that maketh haste to be rich shall not be innocent."

Section K

Lie: Gambling is not addictive, so I can quit gambling any time.
Truth: Gambling can easily become a way of life, a bad habit that is hard to break.
John 8:34 Jesus said, "…Whosoever committeth sin is the servant of sin."

Section L

Lie: I can't stop gambling.
Truth: With God's help, I can stop.
Matthew 19:26 "…with God all things are possible."

This page may be reproduced without change and in its entirety to be used at Discover and Recover Club meetings and for noncommercial Christian purposes without prior permission from the author.

Games of a Gambler   Mary Goloversic Copyright   ©   2020 All rights reserved

Section M

Lie: There's no future for me—I've lost everything gambling.

Truth: God has a purpose for you—He wants you to do good works.

Ephesians 2:10 "For we are his workmanship, created in Christ unto good works…"

This page may be reproduced without change and in its entirety to be used at Discover and Recover Club meetings and for noncommercial Christian purposes without prior permission from the author.

<u>Games of a Gambler</u>   Mary Goloversic Copyright   ©   2020 All rights reserved

GAMBLING WORKSHOP—MEETING

Pass out the materials listed above (pages 207-211).
Leader: **Please look at the information on the pamphlet before we start the workshop.**

WELCOME

Leader: **Welcome to the meeting a Gambling Workshop.**
In this club, we discover God's truths and use these truths to recognize the lies of gambling and apply the truths to our lives.
We will use the handout meeting pages in this way:
The leader reads the sentences in bold print.
The capitalized words in regular print are section dividers and do not have to be read.
Leader and club members read the sentences in regular print.
The other regular print sentences/ phrases in *italics* are directions.

OPENING PRAYER

Leader: **I will begin by reading the opening prayer.**
"Dear God,
Thank you for bringing us together. We

This page may be reproduced without change and in its entirety to be used at Discover and Recover Club meetings and for noncommercial Christian purposes without prior permission from the author.
<u>Games of a Gambler</u>   Mary Goloversic Copyright   ©   2020 All rights reserved

know You are the Most Holy. We love You, God. We are glad You love us, even when we behave badly.

We know we sin—we think bad things, say bad things and do bad things. We are sorry for our sins. Please help up to be better for You.

Please help us to have a good workshop to discover your truths and use them to recover from our gambling habit.

We pray in Jesus' Name, amen."

<u>READINGS FROM BOOK, GAMES OF A GAMBLER—if there is time.</u> (If there is no time, go to Session 1-C)

Leader: **This workshop is based on the book, <u>Games of a Gambler</u>, by Mary Goloversic. The story is about a gambler whose gambling put him in prison. It starts when he gets out of prison and enters temporary housing at a Success House, similar to a halfway house, but with special meeting with 8-step success counselors and attendance at Success Club meetings, Success Workshop, and church. Life at the Success House will help him adjust to being out of prison and prepare him for leading a successful life out of prison by learning God's truths, recognizing lies in his life, and using God's truths to overcome his addiction to gambling.**

This page may be reproduced without change and in its entirety to be used at Discover and Recover Club meetings and for noncommercial Christian purposes without prior permission from the author.

<u>Games of a Gambler</u>   Mary Goloversic Copyright   ©   2020 All rights reserved

We will now read chapters 20 and 21.
We will take turns reading aloud.
If you do not want to read, just say "pass."
I will start the reading.

RECOGNIZING LIES & LEARNING GOD'S TRUTHS

Leader: **Look up box A on your papers. I will use the**
Bible to look up the Scripture in box A and then
read it.
(give the members time to find the paper with box A and then
leader reads the Scripture from the Bible)
Let's all read aloud the information in box A.
(all read this)
Please copy the information in box A.

DISCUSSION QUESTIONS

Leader: **We will now have discussion questions.**
Look at the notes you just copied.
I will read each discussion question and then
please share you answers to each question.

Leader: **Question 1 about past failure:**
What did you ever think or day or do that the lies says?
(members answer the question)

This page may be reproduced without change and in its entirety to be used at Discover and Recover Club meetings and for noncommercial Christian purposes without prior permission from the author.
Games of a Gambler   Mary Goloversic Copyright   ©   2020 All rights reserved

Leader: **Question 2 about past success:**
What did you ever think or say or do that the truth says?
(members answer the question)

Leader: **Question 3 about present success:**
What progress did you make recently?
(members answer the question)

Leader: **Question 4 about plans for more success:**
What do you plan to think or say or do now to carry out the truth in today's information box?
(members answer the question)

Leader and members repeat the above procedure—note-taking and discussion questions—for box B.

Leader and members repeat the above procedure—note-taking and discussion questions for box C.

After box B and Box C area completed, leader says this.
Leader: **We will now take a break and then go on to**
session 2.

GOD—JESUS

Leader: **You need Jesus to help you to stop gambling.**
You need Jesus to get into heaven.

This page may be reproduced without change and in its entirety to be used at Discover and Recover Club meetings and for noncommercial Christian purposes without prior permission from the author.
<u>Games of a Gambler</u>   Mary Goloversic Copyright   ©   2020 All rights reserved

Long ago God, the Father, sent Jesus, His Son, from heaven to earth to shed His blood dying on the cross to cover your sins, to pay for your sins. Listen to God's promise in John 3:16 of the Bible.

"For God so loved the world,
that he have his only begotten Son
that whosoever believeth in him
should not perish,
but have everlasting life."

In I Corinthians 15:1-6 of the Bible, God explains more about what Jesus did.
"...the gospel...

By which also ye are saved...
...how that Christ died for our sins...
And that he was buried, and that he rose again the third day...
And that he was seen...of above five hundred brethren at once..."

John 3:16 says God gave His Son.
God offers YOU payment for your sins by accepting God's Gift—Jesus.
This Gift must be accepted to become YOUR Gift.

This page may be reproduced without change and in its entirety to be used at Discover and Recover Club meetings and for noncommercial Christian purposes without prior permission from the author.

Games of a Gambler   Mary Goloversic Copyright   ©   2020 All rights reserved

Do YOU believe Jesus died for your sins, was buried, and rose again to live with God, the Father, in heaven?
If you do, you can accept Jesus now by praying the prayer I read to you now.
Please bow your heads and close your eyes.
I will pause every few words, so you can silently repeat the words to God.

"**Dear God,** (pause)

I know that I sin. (pause)
I think bad thoughts, (pause) **say bad things,** (pause) **do bad things.** (pause)
I hurt You, others, and myself. (pause)
I am sorry for all my sins. (pause)

I believe Your words in the Bible.
I believe that You sent Jesus (pause) **to die on the cross** *(pause)* **to pay for my sins.** *(pause)*
I believe He was buried, *(pause)* **rose again,** *(pause)* **returned to earth for a while,** *(italics)* **and now lives in heaven.** *(pause)*

I accept Your Gift of Jesus *(pause)* **in payment for my sins** (pause) **and for everlasting life with you.** *(pause)*

This page may be reproduced without change and in its entirety to be used at Discover and Recover Club meetings and for noncommercial Christian purposes without prior permission from the author.
<u>Games of a Gambler</u>   Mary Goloversic Copyright   ©   2020 All rights reserved

Thank You for this Gift of Jesus *(pause)* **for my Savior. In Jesus' Name, amen."** *(pause)*

<u>READINGS FROM BOOK, GAMES OF A GAMBLER—</u> <u>if there is time.</u> (If there is no time, go to session 2-C.)

Leader: **We will now read chapters 15, 16, and 24 of the book, <u>Games of a Gambler</u>.**
We will take turns reading aloud.
If you do not want to read aloud, just say "pass."
I will start the reading.

RECOGNIZING LIES & LEARNING GOD'S TRUTHS

Leader: **Look for box F on your papers.**
I will look up the Scripture in the Bible and read it.
(give members time to find box F and then read the Scripture to them)
Let's all read aloud the information in box F.
(leader and members read it aloud)
Please copy the information in box F.
(allow time for member to copy the information)

DISCUSSION QUESTIONS
Leader: **We will now have discussion on questions.**
Look at the notes you just copied

This page may be reproduced without change and in its entirety to be used at Discover and Recover Club meetings and for noncommercial Christian purposes without prior permission from the author.

<u>Games of a Gambler</u>   Mary Goloversic Copyright   ©   2020 All rights reserved

I will read each discussion question and then please share your answers to each question.

Leader: **<u>Question 1</u>—about your past failure**
What did you ever think or say or do that the lie says?
(allow time for members to answer)

Leader: **Question 2 about past success:**
<u>What did you ever think or say or do that the truth says?</u>
(members answer the question)

Leader: **Question 3 about present success:**
<u>What progress did you make recently?</u>
(members answer the question)

Leader: **Question 4 about plans for more success:**
<u>What do you plan to think or say or do now to carry out the truth in today's information box?</u>
(members answer the question)

Leader and members repeat the above procedure—note-taking and discussion questions—for box H.

Leader and members repeat the above procedure—note-taking and discussion questions for box I.

This page may be reproduced without change and in its entirety to be used at Discover and Recover Club meetings and for noncommercial Christian purposes without prior permission from the author.
<u>Games of a Gambler</u>   Mary Goloversic Copyright   ©   2020 All rights reserved

After box B and Box C area completed, leader says this.
Leader: **We will now take a break and then go on to session 3.**

8 STEPS TO SUCCESS

Leader: **The author of this workshop has written books to guide adults, teens, and children to success.**
She developed the Bible-based 8 Steps to Success.
These steps help anybody to develop a great lifestyle.
The author's defines success as: being the person God wants you to be, not what you or others want you to be.
Now please read aloud these 8 Steps and Scriptures.
(leader and members read the 8 steps)
8 Steps for Success

1. **Read truths in Bible**
   "Search the Scriptures…" John 5:39
2. **Recognize lies**
   "Let no man deceive you…" II Thessalonians 2:3
3. **Repent**
   "…I will be sorry for my sin." Psalm 38:18
4. **Replace**
   "…put off…the old man…put on...the new man…" Ephesians 4:22,24

This page may be reproduced without change and in its entirety to be used at Discover and Recover Club meetings and for noncommercial Christian purposes without prior permission from the author.
Games of a Gambler   Mary Goloversic Copyright   ©   2020 All rights reserved

5. <u>Love</u>
   "…love one another…" John 15:12
6. <u>Forgive</u>
   "…forgiving one another…" Ephesians 4:32
7. <u>Communicate</u>
   "…speaking the truth in love…" Ephesians 4:15
8. <u>Help</u>
   "…come and help…" Luke 5:7

<u>READINGS FROM BOOK, Games of a Gambler—if there is time.</u> (If there is no time, go to session 3-C.)

Leader: **We will now read chapter 25 of the book,
<u>Games of a Gambler</u>.
We will take turns reading aloud.
If you do not want to read aloud, say "pass."
I will start the reading.**

RECOGNIZING LIES & LEARNING GOD'S TRUTHS

Leader: **Look for box K on your papers.
I will look up the Scripture in the Bible and read it.**
(give members time to find box K and then read the Scripture to them)
Let's all read aloud the information in box K.

This page may be reproduced without change and in its entirety to be used at Discover and Recover Club meetings and for noncommercial Christian purposes without prior permission from the author.

<u>Games of a Gambler</u>   Mary Goloversic Copyright   ©   2020 All rights reserved

(leader and members read it aloud)
Please copy the information in box K.
(allow time for member to copy the information)

DISCUSSION QUESTIONS

Leader: **We will now have discussion on questions.**
Look at the notes you just copied
I will read each discussion question and then
please share your answers to each question.

Leader: **Question 1—about your past failure**
What did you ever think or say or do that the lie
says?
(allow time for members to answer)

Leader: **Question 2 about past success:**
What did you ever think or say or do that the truth says?
(members answer the question)

Leader: **Question 3 about present success:**
What progress did you make recently?
(members answer the question)

Leader: **Question 4 about plans for more success:**
What do you plan to think or say or do now to carry out
the truth in today's information box?
(members answer the question)

This page may be reproduced without change and in its entirety to be used at Discover and Recover Club meetings and for noncommercial Christian purposes without prior permission from the author.

<u>Games of a Gambler</u>   Mary Goloversic Copyright   ©   2020 All rights reserved

Leader and members repeat the above procedure—note-taking and discussion questions—for box L.

Leader and members repeat the above procedure—note-taking and discussion questions for box M.

CLOSING OF GAMBLING WORKSHOP

Leader: **Thank you for coming to this workshop.
Please bow your heads and look at this prayer.
If you want to confess YOUR sin of gambling to God,
silently read this prayer while I read the prayer aloud.**
(read the confession prayer aloud)

**Dear God,
I realize I was wrong to gamble. I misused Your money by losing it gambling and helped others misuse Your money by winning money from them. I am sorry for gambling.**

Keeping your heads bowed, please close your eyes while I read the closing prayer.
(read the closing prayer)

**"Dear God,
Thank You for Your truths in the Bible to guide us to break the habit of gambling. Thank you for any progress we have made.**

This page may be reproduced without change and in its entirety to be used at Discover and Recover Club meetings and for noncommercial Christian purposes without prior permission from the author.
Games of a Gambler   Mary Goloversic Copyright   ©   2020 All rights reserved

Help us to keep private the confidential comments people shared today. Help as we apply Your Truths found in today's Scripture.

Please give us strength to say 'no' to gambling.

Help us keep looking up to You.

In Jesus' Name, amen."

This page may be reproduced without change and in its entirety to be used at Discover and Recover Club meetings and for noncommercial Christian purposes without prior permission from the author.

<u>Games of a Gambler</u>   Mary Goloversic Copyright   ©   2020 All rights reserved

SUCCESS AND SALVATION PAMPHLET

**success = being the person God wants you to be,
not what you or others want you to be.**

<u>**8 Steps for Success**</u>

1. <u>**Read truths in Bible**</u>
   "Search the Scriptures..." John 5:39
2. <u>**Recognize lies**</u>
   "Let no man deceive you..." II Thessalonians 2:3
3. <u>**Repent**</u>
   "...I will be sorry for my sin." Psalm 38:18
4. <u>**Replace**</u>
   "...put off...the old man...put on...the new man..."
   Ephesians 4:22,24
5. <u>**Love**</u>
   "...love one another..." John 15:12
6. <u>**Forgive**</u>
   "...forgiving one another..." Ephesians 4:32
7. <u>**Communicate**</u>
   "...speaking the truth in love..." Ephesians 4:15
8. <u>**Help**</u>
   "...come and help..." Luke 5:7

<u>**Jesus is needed to be successful. You need Jesus.**</u>

<u>**Believe this Bible verse:**</u>
"For God so loved the world, that he gave his only begotten Son, that whosoever believeth in him should not perish, but have everlasting life." John 3:16

<u>**Pray a prayer like this:**</u>
Dear God, I sin. I am sorry I sinned. I believe Jesus died on the cross to pay for my sins and He rose again. I accept Jesus as my Savior. Thank you."

This page may be reproduced without change and in its entirety to be used at Discover and Recover Club meetings and for noncommercial Christian purposes without prior permission from the author.

<u>Games of a Gambler</u>   Mary Goloversic Copyright   ©   2020 All rights reserved

This page may be reproduced without change and in its entirety to be used at Discover and Recover Club meetings and for noncommercial Christian purposes without prior permission from the author.

<u>Games of a Gambler</u>   Mary Goloversic Copyright   ©   2020 All rights reserved

Printed in the United States
By Bookmasters